Dear Reader:

There are some decisions in life that a human being dreads ever having to make. On the top of that list is the decision to save one person's life over another's. The pain and anguish increases ten-fold when the lives are those of children. In *Nina's Got a Secret*, that is exactly what the main female character must decide; which child's life to save. In this gripping tale of love, secrets, and drama, Brian W. Smith takes readers on a thrill ride full of suspense and intrigue.

Some people get married for love. Some people get married for security. Some people get married for sheer convenience. At the end of the day, they have still made a commitment that their partner expects them to keep. But often both spouses may be hiding a secret and things are rarely as they seem. What happens when carefully laid plans and unrealistic expectations begin to unravel, when friendship turns to blackmail and jealousy, when everyone has an end game plan of their own is told within the pages of *Nina's Got a Secret*. I am sure you will enjoy it.

As always, thanks for supporting the efforts of Strebor Books. We strive to bring you fresh, talented and ground-breaking authors that will help you escape reality when the daily stressors of life seem overwhelming. We appreciate the love and dedication of our readers. You can find all of our titles on the Internet at www.zanestore.com and you can find me on eroticanoir.com or Facebook.com/AuthorZane.

Blessings,

Zane

Publisher
Strebor Books International
www.simonandschuster.com/streborbooks

ZANE PRESENTS

Nina's
GOT A
SECRET

BRIAN W. SMITH

SBI
STREBOR BOOKS
NEW YORK LONDON TORONTO SYDNEY

SBI

Strebor Books
P.O. Box 6505
Largo, MD 20792
http://www.streborbooks.com

© 2012 by Brian W. Smith

ISBN 978-1-59309-412-6
ISBN 978-1-4516-5744-9 (e-book)
LCCN 2011938329

First Strebor Books trade paperback edition September 2012

Cover design: www.mariondesigns.com
Cover photograph: © Keith Saunders/Marion Designs

10 9 8 7 6 5 4 3 2 1

Manufactured in the United States of America

For information regarding special discounts for bulk purchases,
please contact Simon & Schuster Special Sales at 1-866-506-1949
or business@simonandschuster.com

The Simon & Schuster Speakers Bureau can bring authors to your
live event. For more information or to book an event, contact the
Simon & Schuster Speakers Bureau at 1-866-248-3049 or visit our
website at www.simonspeakers.com.

ACKNOWLEDGMENTS

I'd like to thank God for continuing to bless me the way he has—even when I fail to acknowledge his power or understand some of the things that have happened in my life. I'd like to thank my family for always supporting me. To the readers—especially the book clubs—who have supported me throughout my career, I say thank you.

Last, but certainly not least, I'd like to thank Zane for giving me the opportunity to join the Strebor team.

"To subdue the enemy's army without fighting is the acme of skill."
—Sun Tzu, *The Art of War*

# PROLOGUE

No matter how much forewarning a person is given to prepare for the death of a family member, rarely is the allocated time enough. Sure, we try to be strong by being proactive in our preparation. We secure insurance policies and put them in a safe place where they're accessible and easy to retrieve. Some people even take their emotional maturity to another level by writing the eulogy before the ailing person dies…that's what Larry did in an effort to prepare for his wife, Deidra's, death.

Unfortunately, Larry learned the hard way that trying to prepare for the death of a loved one is a lot like the description Mike Tyson once gave a young reporter during a crowded press conference.

The young reporter stood in the back of the room and boldly blurted out, "Mike, your opponent says he has a good plan on how to beat you."

Mike looked at the young reporter with his trademark scowl and profoundly replied, "Everybody's got a plan—until they get hit."

No one ever said Iron Mike was the sharpest pencil in the box, but that was a very profound statement. It's a statement that perfectly describes the issue of death. Mike's comment captures what death does to us all; it punches us in the face until our eyes water and forces us to suddenly forget our so-called *plans* for dealing with it.

Deidra was diagnosed with inoperable brain cancer a few months after she gave birth to their daughter, Chrissy. When the hospice nurse, Maxine, visited on the day Deidra's life expired, she didn't have to tell Larry that Deidra had a few hours left. The normally poised Maxine seemed on edge as she checked Deidra's pulse and adjusted the gauges on her breathing apparatus. For weeks she'd eagerly given Larry a detailed prognosis on his wife's condition, but on this final day, she avoided looking into Larry's eyes—a behavioral change Larry quickly picked up on.

As the nurse backed her car out of the driveway, Larry could feel his heart flutter. His mouth became dry as his nerves started to seize control of his body as he stared helplessly out of the window and watched the nurse drive away.

Larry was usually poised and in total control of his emotions, but he could feel himself starting to lose it. His body became jittery and his hands began to tremble as he searched for the intestinal fortitude he would need to control his feelings. If only there was a button he could push, or a magic potion he could drink, to help stop the emotional roller coaster that raged out of control within him.

He could hear his friends and family members in the living room. As more arrived, their murmurs grew louder. Occasional sounds of laughter were usually followed by crying sounds. They were usually followed by words of consolation.

There is an old saying: *"Pressure doesn't create character, it reveals character."* Never is this saying truer than when there is an impending death in the family.

When pressure kicks in, most of us seek refuge in the emotional bunkers we are most comfortable with. The specter of death illuminates this fact. You can bet your paycheck that whatever personality traits a person displays during calmer times will become much more pronounced when the unpleasant aspects of life show up at the door.

The family clown will do all he/she can to entertain. The family's Bible-toting Christian will do all he/she can to be viewed as the spiritual backbone. That one sneaky money-grubbing family member will slip away into a bedroom and start rummaging through drawers and file cabinets in search of insurance policies he/she has absolutely no right to look at. Last, but not least, the family's designated "passer outer"—the person that starts screaming and faints at everyone's funeral—will do what "passer outers" do: pass the fuck out.

While everyone congregated in the next room, playing their roles to a tee, Larry reached and grabbed his wife's cold hand. Deidra was hanging on for dear life, but her extremities were beginning to resemble that of a corpse. She'd lost so much weight that her face looked skeletal. Her veins were protruding from her skin like little purple tubes.

As Larry slowly slid his fingers across Deidra's knuckles, he shared his thoughts with his wife. "Well, baby, I guess I'm gonna have to do this parenting thing on my own. You know you're wrong for leaving me hanging like this. We always said that we would grow old together, but it doesn't look like that's going to work out the way we planned.

"Can you believe that the baby we struggled to conceive is about to turn a year old? I can tell that she's going to be just like you when she gets older. I'm going to make sure there are always reminders of you around so that she will never forget your beautiful face.

"Sweetheart, I know you're tired. I know you've been trying to hang in there and be strong for Chrissy and me, but I want you to know that it's okay. I'm going to take care of our baby. I will protect her with my life if I have to.

"I want you to go ahead and sleep. Get your rest. Just know that Chrissy and I are going to be okay. Know that we love you with all of our hearts, and that we will never forget you, baby. We love you—I love you."

The tears Larry had been struggling to hold back finally escaped his eyes and cascaded down his cheeks. He'd been the picture of strength since Deidra was initially diagnosed, but all dams—whether they are physical or emotional—are subject to collapse.

Larry's first emotional meltdown came swiftly and with the ferociousness of the floodwaters that spilled over the levees in New Orleans during Hurricane Katrina. He felt helpless each day as he watched Deidra's corneas take on a different hue and the whites of her eyeballs become less visible because of her sagging eyelids. His inability to change her destiny caused him to revisit an old childhood habit of biting his fingernails. When Larry was a kid, he often nibbled on his fingernails and fingertips when he was nervous. He hadn't engaged in the nasty habit in nearly twenty years, but his grief caused him to rely on any coping mechanism he could think of. With each passing day, his habit became worse. By the time Maxine departed for the last time, the tips of Larry's index fingers and the cuticles around his thumbs looked like they'd been gnawed on by parasites.

Signs of the erosion of Larry's emotional state were obvious in other ways. He'd been so consumed with Deidra's care that his own hygiene was suffering, an odd occurrence for a man who normally took great pride in his appearance. Realizing that his body odor and the smell of Deidra's body fluids had combined to create a stench in the room, Larry decided that washing up right there on the spot was better than spending even one second away from Deidra's side. He poured the remains from a water bottle on a towel and scrubbed his underarms non-stop for more than ten minutes, pausing long enough to allow the burning sensation produced by the friction to subside. He followed up this odd way of bathing by dowsing his underarms with powder.

Comfortable with the fresh smell emanating from his armpits, he reached back and locked the door to his bed-room as he finally let the tears he'd been holding back flow. His older sister, Barbara, the family Bible toter, knocked hard and pleaded for him to let her in, but he ignored her and buried his head into Deidra's covers.

Larry allowed himself to have one of those deep, heart-felt cries. It was the kind of cry that originated in the lower diaphragm and gushed out like oil from a rig. These moments may happen once or twice in a man's life, and when they happen, the only worthwhile and effective con-solation is solitude.

Interestingly enough, the sound of his emotions and Barbara's banging on the door didn't stop Larry from noticing the absence of the most important sound in the room. The sound was so subtle that most people would have missed it, but its absence was enough to make Larry stop crying. It was a sound Larry had grown accustomed to hearing during the three weeks that Deidra lay in the house receiving medical care from Maxine.

An oxygen tank sat a few feet away from Deidra's bed. A thin tube ran from the top of the tank and into Deidra's nostrils. It was her lifeline. As the days passed, it became increasingly difficult for Deidra to breathe. Every few seconds, she could be heard taking a breath as she struggled to garner as much oxygen as her fluid-filled lungs could handle. It sounded like someone with the permanent sniffles.

While sitting next to Deidra's bed during the course of the three weeks, Larry actually started anticipating the sniffs. He monitored the sniffs so closely that he could tell when Deidra's time was running out because the sniffs starting coming quicker. The shorter time between sniffs was an indication of how difficult it had become for her to breathe.

While he sat slouched in the chair next to her bed sobbing uncontrollably, Larry attempted to dry his eyes once he noticed that the sniffs he'd grown to anticipate suddenly stopped. There was no sound. The room grew cold. His wife's vein-covered, frigid hand was now lifeless. Deidra was gone. Larry was now a widower.

Two Thousand Miles Away On That Same Day...

Nina sat on the battered hardwood floor of her mouse-infested, one-bedroom "shotgun" house and clipped coupons. She looked like a little Native American girl as she sat with her legs crossed and her wavy black hair pulled back into one long braid.

Nina took great pride in her coupon collection. She could be a perfectionist at times, and it showed in the way she carefully cut along the dotted lines of the coupons she chose. Afterward, she would painstakingly separate the old from the new, the cereals from the drinks, and the 20% off coupons from the 10% off coupons. NASA scientists didn't display this type of attention to detail.

Although she focused hard on her task, she kept a watchful eye on her ten-month-old daughter, Precious, who lay sleeping on a blanket a few feet away. The child had just dozed off, so Nina was careful not to make any sudden moves that would startle her light-sleeping and overly-observant infant.

The beat-up 20-inch television was positioned a few

feet in front of her on a rickety, particle-board stand. Nina was able to ignore the distorted picture because the television's primary purpose was to serve as a source of light for the room. Nina had learned to not rely on the television for entertainment because the picture was extremely snowy and the remote control was missing buttons, making it impossible to change the channels.

With the television permanently set on Channel 4, Nina focused on her coupons and occasionally glanced at the local news. She didn't pay much attention to the news report until she heard the reporter announce, *"Two African-American males found shot to death in a drive-by shooting that appeared to be drug-related."*

Nina allowed the old rusty scissors she was using to rest for a moment as she squinted to try to see the reporter on the ashy screen. She inched closer to the screen to get a better view of the live broadcast. Suddenly, the ash on the screen gave way just long enough for her to notice that the bullet-riddled car in the background behind the news reporter looked a lot like the car Flip, her child's father, drove.

As angst started to invade her senses, Nina applied the universal hood technical support strategy to the television to fix the picture. She smacked the television a few times on the side and shook it until the picture started to show better. Much to her chagrin, the clearer the picture became, the deeper she would plummet in the porthole to a pain she would never shake.

Nina placed her hands over her mouth and stumbled backward as the reporter announced the name of the victims. *"Bystanders identified one of the victims as twenty-one-year-old Donald 'Flip' LeBlanc."*

The coupons that Nina had carefully stacked in three separate piles were stepped on and now scattered all over the floor as Nina wandered aimlessly in the tiny room. Her need for physical support prompted Nina to immediately pick Precious up and squeeze her tightly. She hugged the child until she awakened. Unaware that her father had just been murdered, Precious did what any startled baby would do after being awakened from a sound sleep: she started crying.

Nina stood there holding her child in the middle of the room and cried along with the baby. It was as if time stood still. They were all alone. Their bond as mother and daughter instantly magnified.

Before she could put Precious into the crib and turn the volume up on the television, Nina's phone started to ring excessively. Nina didn't bother to answer. The angst that invaded her body when she first saw the car on television had mutated into an emotional pain that was so heavy and hurtful it made her knees buckle.

Once Nina collapsed and fell to the floor, answering the phone was no longer an option. At that point, Nina didn't care. She knew that it would be her so-called friends notifying her of what she already knew: the love of her life was dead.

CHAPTER ONE

MAY 14, 2008

Despite all of the hoopla surrounding a wedding day, more often than not, the people jumping the broom usually have less fun than the curious guests attending the ceremony. When it's your wedding day, glee and unbridled joy is often replaced with tension. The type of smile that's customary for such a festive occasion is stored away until after the ceremony. Even the poise needed to embrace last-minute snafus and unexpected occurrences is usually lost and nowhere to be found.

The church where Larry and Nina gathered for their nuptials was impressive. The Mercedes limousine that was parked outside waiting to whisk the new couple away was equally impressive. There was no shortage of guests there to see this odd union. But, all of the pomp and circumstance in the world can't hide a lack of sincerity from the primary participants. A fact Larry would be forced to come face-to-face with.

The thing that made the union between Larry Dennison and Nina Arceneaux so unique was that the roles were totally and unmistakably reversed. Traditionally, it's the woman who is irritable and difficult to get along with on the day of the wedding. It's the woman who is more concerned about the decorations and whether the minister is on time. It's the woman who is wasting time badgering the wedding coordinator about the seating arrangements when she should be getting her hair primped. Stereotypical roles weren't to be in this union.

"Larry, you need to calm down, my brotha," said Terry, Larry's best man.

"Man, I just want everything to be right. Do you have the ring?"

"For the fifth time, yes, I have the ring!"

"Okay. I just want this to be perfect. I really want this to be a special day for Nina."

"Dog, just relax. I've already had the wedding coordinator double and triple check everything. All you need to do is get ready to grab your nuts, kiss your days as a bachelor goodbye, and marry that woman."

Larry stared in the mirror and looked at his tuxedo once again. Sweat beads started to form as he struggled to pluck a pesky piece of lint off of his shoulder.

"Dog, are you absolutely sure you wanna do this?" Terry asked.

"Yep, so don't ask me that again."

"All right, my brotha," Terry said, as he stood behind the nervous groom and put his hands on his shoulders. "I just wanna make sure you got your head on straight.

My instincts are tellin' me that this may not be a good move."

"Trust me, dog, my head is on as straight as it's ever been," Larry replied, opting to look at Terry through the mirror rather than turn around. "Nina and I are meant to be together. We are in love with each other. We get along great, and I love her daughter like she was my own. She supports me and my career; and the fact that she is finer than Beyoncé doesn't hurt.

"I am ready to marry this woman. Now, can you stop being a detective long enough to be happy for me and be my best man?"

"I can respect that," Terry replied. "I'm not a police detective today. I'm just your boy."

"I hope you got your head on straight," said a burly female voice. It was Larry's sister, Barbara.

She walked into the room wearing a blue sequined dress, matching hat, and a frown on her face. By the way she was frowning and squinting, you would have thought she'd just eaten an onion and washed it down with a glass of prune juice.

The scowl lines that resided on her forehead stretched and curved until they made their way down to the space between her eyebrows. There was no mistaking her feelings regarding the nuptials that would soon take place.

Rarely did anyone pay much attention to Barbara because her temperament was usually unpleasant. Her nickname should have been *Bad Mood*. One of Larry's friends once described her as the mean high school vice principal that roamed the hallways pissed off at all the students because she got passed over once again for a principal position.

Larry rolled his eyes when he saw Barbara come into the room. Her negativity was the one thing he didn't want to deal with on his wedding day. He instinctively knew that the only way he could avoid allowing her sour mood to taint this special day was to make sure she remained occupied at all times.

"Barb, don't start messin' with me."

"I didn't say a thing."

"You don't have to say anything; it's written all over your face."

"I don't know what you're talkin' 'bout," Barbara replied as she used her long nails to remove that elusive piece of lint Larry was battling. "So tell me, baby brother, is Ms. Nina going to take on your last name?"

"I told you last week what the plan was. She doesn't have any brothers to carry on her family name. Besides, she doesn't want her daughter to have to grow up answering questions about having a different last name than her mother."

"So, what you're saying is she's going to be one of these women that put the hyphen between their maiden and their married name."

"Yes, Barbara! That's what I'm saying. Now leave it alone."

"Man, I'm tellin' you now, when I get married, the only way my wife will be keeping her maiden name is if she's some kind of movie star or celebrity and she makes money off of her maiden name. If that's not the case, she's ridin' with me 100 percent," Terry said.

"Hello!" Barbara shouted.

"Leave it alone," Larry said with a growl as he glared over at Terry.

"All right," Terry replied. "I'ma go and see what's happening out there."

"You should follow him, Barbara."

"I'd prefer to stay here and help you."

"Sis, I don't need your help. If you wanna help me, go and check on Nina. I know she's probably nervous. She doesn't have a ton of relatives and friends here to support her."

"She has her bridesmaids."

"I know that, but it would mean a lot to me if you went over and offered to help her. Do that for me, Barb."

Barbara sighed and rolled her eyes. She wasn't Nina's biggest fan, and she wasn't shy about letting her brother know it. As far as she was concerned, Nina may have been a lot of things, but good enough for her brother wasn't one of them.

She kissed Larry on the cheek and then slapped him upside the head as she reluctantly left the room and headed over to Nina's dressing room.

It was Nina's wedding day, but you wouldn't have known it by the somber look on her face. Nina was the type of self-centered diva who would spend three months co-ordinating the outfit she was going to wear to her eight-year-old daughter's birthday party. Considering the size of her ego, her lack of excitement about her own wedding was a clear sign to her best friend, Val, that Nina didn't really want to go through with this ceremony.

"Nina, are you sure you want to do this?"

"Val, that's the third time you've asked me that today."

"And I'm gonna keep asking you until you give me an honest answer," Val replied as she sat in the high back chair in the corner of the room. "Nina, you don't have to marry this man."

"I know that."

"So why are you doing this?"

"Why do you think I'm going to marry him?"

"I don't know. He is shorter than you."

"What does his height have to do with this?"

"Nina, you know damn well you ain't lookin' forward to being the tallest nigga in the bed. Besides, you've already admitted that you aren't physically attracted to him and you don't love him. He's nearly ten years older than you. You've already admitted that he's got a little dick and he doesn't eat pussy. So, I can only conclude that you're about to marry this man because he has money."

"Ahhh, excuse me, have you forgotten that we are in a church?"

"My bad," Val sheepishly replied.

"The money doesn't hurt. My child and I can use the financial stability."

"Nina, that doesn't make any damn sense!" Val blurted out, forgetting to censor her language in the church. "You were the most attractive dancer in that club. You used to make more money than most of us combined. You don't need his money."

"Val, I couldn't be a stripper forever. The money was good, but I'm damn near thirty years old."

"Yeah, damn near thirty years old with the body of a twenty-year-old and a face like a model. I don't get it. I've seen fine-ass athletes and actors come into that club and practically beg you to marry them."

"What's your point?"

"My point is you can do better! While the rest of us were shaking our asses off just to get twenty-dollar bills, you were around there flashing a smile and getting hundred-dollar bills shoved in your hands on the regular. I just don't understand why you've suddenly decided to hook up with the Pillsbury Doughboy."

"It's not about the way he looks. Larry loves me."

"No, he's obsessed with you. He's been tryin' to buy your affection. He came to that club like clockwork for two straight years looking for you. The man wouldn't accept a dance or give his money to anyone but you. I can remember when he came into the club one day looking for you and you weren't there. The poor thing looked like he was about to start crying."

"He treats me better than any man has ever treated

me, and he treats my daughter like she was his own child."

"I ain't stupid! I know the fact that he has all those Hollywood connections has somethin' to do with this. You're doin' this for the wrong reasons!"

"Is it wrong for me to want to make sure my daughter has more than I ever had? Is it wrong for me to not want my daughter to have to sit around and collect coupons before she goes to the grocery store? Should I apologize for marrying someone who can provide opportunities for me and my child?"

"Girl, you act like he's your savior or something."

"I don't know about all that, but he did save my life."

"What do you mean?"

Nina stopped looking in the mirror while she brushed her long flowing hair, and turned around in her chair to face Val.

"Vee, I've never told you this, but he literally saved my life. Do you know that football player they call 'Big Red' that used to come to the club all the time?"

"Yeah, I remember him. What happened to him? He used to come there and *make it rain* with hundred-dollar bills. I haven't seen him in a year."

"There's a reason why he no longer comes to the club. Last summer when you took some time off after your surgery, Big Red came into the club and offered me two hundred dollars for a lap dance. I was cool with that, but once we got into the private room he started acting strange. He started feeling on me, and tried to slide his finger inside my thong, so I got up and tried to leave. He grabbed my arm and offered me five hundred if I gave him a blowjob. When I told him no, he offered me a thousand dollars. I told him he had the wrong girl and tried to walk out, but he pushed me up against the wall. When I tried to move toward the door, he slapped me in the face."

"You're lying!" Val replied as she covered her mouth in astonishment.

"I wish I was. Val, he hit me so hard I was literally seeing stars. I tried to get up off the ground, but I couldn't. When I finally made it to my knees, I looked up and all I could see was a knife pointed in my face. He unzipped his pants and then grabbed my hair."

"What happened?" Val asked as she moved closer to Nina.

"He pulled out his dick and was about to force me to suck it. I was so scared of him I was about to do it. But suddenly I heard glass shattering and Big Red went stumbling across the room, his dick still in his hand."

"What happened?"

"Larry came into the room and hit Big Red in the back of his head with a wine bottle."

"I'm surprised Big Red didn't try to hurt him."

"That's the first thing I thought. Larry grabbed me and led me back to our dressing room. He helped me clean out my locker and brought me home. I haven't been back to that club since."

"Damn, I didn't know it went down like that. So, that's why you quit dancing. I knew there was more to it than what you told all of us. Shit, I'm supposed to be your best friend; you could've told me the truth."

"I was too embarrassed."

"You used to enjoy dancing too much to suddenly quit the way you did."

"Girl, for the past year, he has taken care of all of my needs. It was that incident that let me know just how much clout Larry had. He's one of the most powerful sports agents in the game. A few days after the incident, Larry called Big Red's agent and went ballistic on the phone. About a week after that, I came home from the gym and sitting on my porch was a dozen roses and a beautifully wrapped box. Val, my mouth dropped when I opened up the box."

"What was in it?"

"There was twenty thousand dollars in cash inside of that box. When I showed Larry the box of money, he looked at me and said, *'That's how professional athletes apologize,'* and then he turned and walked away."

"Daaaamn!" Val said with a grin.

"Tell me about it! Val, I'm not gonna lie, that shit turned me on."

"I'll bet it did. I'm getting turned on right now."

"We've been together ever since."

"Well, since you put it like that, I can understand. I don't know how you're going to deal with the fact that you're not truly in love with him, but I guess you can work around that. The man has definitely got your back."

"I know he does. That's why I'm comfortable marrying him. I may not love him now, but eventually I'll learn to love him."

"It's not just him you're going to have to *learn* to love; you're going to have to love his daughter. Doesn't she have autism?"

"Yeah," Nina replied and then turned back around and started brushing her hair again.

"How old is she?"

"She's eight years old. She and Precious are roughly the same age. I know that's going to be tough. It's hard enough trying to deal with Precious and all of her moods and bad habits. I'm going to need some help playing mama to an eight-year-old child with autism."

"How long has he had custody of…what's her name again?"

"Her name is Christine, but he calls her Chrissy. He's been raising her on his own since his first wife died eight years ago. Did I tell you she died on the same day that Flip died?"

"No, you didn't tell me that. That's eerie."

"Tell me about it. Anyway, lately, it's been hard for him to do it by himself since his career is booming."

"Do what by himself?"

"Raise Chrissy! He's been struggling to care for her the way she needs to be cared for. He has so many high-profile and demanding clients now, he's having a difficult time giving her the attention she needs; especially since he's been spending so much time in the South and here in Louisiana. Larry told me that we're going to get a live-in nanny when we move to California. Hopefully, that will make the situation more bearable."

"Well, girlfriend, I guess I have a better understanding of what your thoughts are now that you've broken it down for me. I still don't think you should go through with this, but I support your decision."

"Thanks, Val. I need your support. You are the only family I have."

Unbeknownst to Nina and Val, a set of ears was pressed against the door listening to their conversation. The ears belonged to Barbara, and needless to say, she was not pleased with what she'd just heard.

Since their parents died a few years earlier, Barbara took her role as older sibling more serious. She did everything she could to protect and support Larry. She babysat Chrissy, cleaned Larry's house, and washed his clothes. She was a widow with no kids; therefore, her younger brother and niece became the center of her universe.

Barbara nearly twisted her ankle as she ran to tell Larry the truth about his soon-to-be wife. This was the proof she needed to convince her brother to call the wedding off.

"Larry, we need to talk," she shouted as she burst through his dressing room door.

"What's going on, sis? Why aren't you helping Nina get ready?"

"That's what we need to talk about," Barbara replied, struggling to catch her breath.

Terry came back into the room. "Man, those people seem to be getting a little restless. Are you ready?"

"Terry, could you give my brother and me a few minutes alone?"

Terry quickly picked up on the consternation in Barbara's voice. He turned and left the room immediately.

"What's wrong?"

"Larry, you can't marry this woman. I've felt this way since you first announced your engagement to her, but now I'm convinced."

"Where is this coming from? I thought you were happy for me."

"Larry, you are my little brother, my only brother. I can't stand by and watch you make the biggest mistake of your life."

"Barb, I love this woman."

"You may love her, but she isn't in love with you, Larry. I just overheard her and her little stripper friend in the room talking."

"So that's what this is about. You still can't get past the fact that Nina used to be a stripper. You won't be satisfied unless I marry someone who is a Bible-toting Christian like you. You want me to be with someone who goes to Sunday School every week, can speak in tongues, and is in four or five different ministries at the church."

"Larry, I won't deny that I would like for you to marry a more spiritual woman. You know that's what Mama and

Daddy would have wanted. But the fact of the matter is, I would support you marrying anyone whom I felt really loved you for your mind and not your money."

"Barbara, I love you, but you are out of line."

"Maybe I am, but I would be mad at myself if I didn't tell you what I just heard."

"What did you hear?"

"I heard Nina say that she could *learn* to love you. Larry, you deserve better. More importantly, my niece deserves a stepmother who genuinely cares about her. Nina couldn't care less about being a mother to Chrissy."

"Barb, I don't need to hear all of this one hour before my wedding. Besides, Nina has always been good to Chrissy, just like I've been good to her daughter, Precious."

"No, Larry. Nina tolerates Chrissy; there's a difference. Chrissy has special needs and I don't think Nina is equipped to take on that responsibility. Baby, she's just happy you took her out of the strip club. Please, sweetie, I'm begging you, don't marry this woman."

Larry finished adjusting his tie in the mirror and then he turned to look at his sister. Barbara had always been his biggest supporter. Rarely did she ever question his decisions, which is why Larry was unwilling to totally ignore her protest. He believed Barbara when she said she overheard Nina making those remarks, but he couldn't change the fact that he was captivated by Nina.

As he stood there watching his sister's eyes fill with water, Larry could feel his pride and his heart at war.

Barbara's information wasn't anything new to Larry. He knew Nina wasn't in love with him, but when it came to love, his heart was stubborn.

"Barbara, I'm marrying Nina, whether you like it or not," Larry finally stated in a low tone, and then walked into the bathroom and closed the door behind him.

To understand his determination to wed the beautiful Nina Arcenaux, you'd have to understand the weird circumstances surrounding how they first met.

Larry became smitten with Nina the moment he saw her dancing on stage. His heart was seized by her beauty, her voluptuous body, and the sensuality she displayed. She seemed to ignore all of the other men in the club and focused solely on him.

After fantasizing about her for nearly two years, he finally won the heart of the most beautiful woman he'd ever seen. Nina's attention was the only thing that helped him move past the pain that lingered from his former wife's death.

Larry would be the first to admit that Nina was rough around the edges. Prior to meeting him, she didn't know how to identify the salad fork at the dinner table. She had never experienced a man opening and closing a door for her. Nina had never traveled on an airplane or even knew what a passport looked like. She was the kind of woman whose good looks and figure afforded her the luxury of being less refined.

Growing up in the rough St. Bernard housing projects

in New Orleans, Nina wasn't exposed to etiquette classes. Her idea of a nice dinner was eating a plate of her grandmother's jambalaya and drinking a large cup of ice-cold grape Kool-Aid as she sat on the second-floor balcony and watched the drug dealers, thugs, and winos scurry beneath.

At the age of two, Nina became the custodial child of her grandmother after her nineteen-year-old mother was killed by her boyfriend. Nina spent the next fifteen years of her life in a constant search for peace. Her teenage body developed faster than her maturity level. As a result, she was ill-equipped to handle the barrage of propositions she received from boys her age, young men that stalked her, and many of the men in her neighborhood who were old enough to be her father.

The verbal harassment she endured during her walk from school to her home was so vile it would have made the most sanctified woman go postal. Getting her butt rubbed and fondled by the sordid men in her community was an unwelcomed but integral part of her travels.

Even if Nina did manage to avoid the scum that dwelled throughout the streets within her ZIP code, she was usually met at her front door by yet another dark secret. Nina's perverted thirty-six-year-old, registered sex-offender uncle lived with them. He honed his molestation skills by sexually abusing her two and sometimes three times a week.

Nina graduated high school on a sunny Friday afternoon,

and less than twenty-four hours later, her clothes were packed and she was gone. She was no longer a boarder in her grandmother's tiny project apartment. She became a tenant of the streets.

That entire summer was spent in transient mode as she lived with various friends until she and her boyfriend, Flip, were able to secure a small one-bedroom apartment.

Flip was just another wannabe drug dealer. He was tall and lanky, and had little to no education. But he had a genuine respect for Nina and eyes that made her weak in the knees whenever he stared at her. He protected her from the scum of the streets as much as he could. He pampered her hood style by making sure he sold enough rocks to guarantee that her hair and nails were always done.

After two months of sleeping on a borrowed mattress and sitting on a hand-me-down sofa, Flip took Nina to the discount furniture store and let her choose her own particle-board, gold-trimmed, five-piece, black lacquer bedroom set. In Nina's eyes, Flip was ballin'.

For his generosity, Nina gave Flip a seven-pound, two-ounce, beautiful baby girl that he insisted be named Precious. Their dream of one day becoming a prosperous family and moving into a house in the suburbs appeared clear and attainable. The thought of being able to walk down streets littered with manicured front lawns instead of empty liquor bottles was a great motivator for both of them. The young couple eagerly put their dreams on the backburner while they stockpiled their cash and made their plans.

Unfortunately, Flip's untimely death changed everything. Without his support, Nina felt lost. He didn't have a duffle bag full of money stashed under the bed like the drug dealers on television. She had no insurance policy to help pay for his funeral or bereavement counseling. She had no family to rely on; only a few people she called friends, and little to no hope.

As she left another interview for a minimum wage job—an interview that she had to once again bring Precious along on because she didn't have a babysitter—she walked past a construction site pushing her daughter in her stroller. Despite her determination to ignore the lustful stares, Nina heard one of the workers yell, *"Girl, you're so fine I'd give you my check on payday if you'd give me a lap dance."*

That idiot's comments garnered laughter from his idiotic peers, but Nina's curiosity was piqued by the suggestion. She always knew that she had the type of beautiful looks and shapely figure that drove men wild. As much as she wanted to live a regular life while working a regular 9-to-5 job, the realization that she was a card-carrying member of the underclass forced her to consider all of her options, including giving lap dances for cash.

Idle thoughts of earning extra money shaking her posterior led to her dropping Precious off at the next-door neighbor's house while she interviewed with the owner of the Wet Dreams strip club.

Donnie, the new club manager, gave her the inaugural tour. It wasn't long before Nina was feeling sick to her stomach. Nina held her breath and said a silent prayer as she braved the cigarette smoke that lingered in the air. She could feel her ass being groped as she strolled past the myriad of hands belonging to the perverts, deadbeats, and jobless patrons that sat around languorously in a strip club at eleven o'clock on a Wednesday morning.

"Baby, you're gonna have to get used to that in here. If you can't handle a little touchy-feely, you need to let me know now," said Donnie as he gnawed on a nasty-looking cigar and opened the door to the dressing room.

"I can handle it," Nina replied as she fought back tears.

And handle it she did. By the end of her first week of work, Nina's physical features catapulted her to the top of the stripper heap. Many of her coworkers envied her ability to mesmerize the clients with little to no effort. It wasn't long before she became a big fish in a very small pond.

Nina eventually earned enough money to move into a decent apartment in eastern New Orleans. The roaches were smaller than the ones that walked and flew around daily in her first apartment. The mice were a welcomed change from the rats she was once accustomed to and had to chase from out of Precious' crib. Most importantly, the stray bullets that were launched from the barrels of automatic handguns being held by niggas with poor aim seemed to be a thing of the past.

But make no mistake about it; the violence of the rough

New Orleans streets is hard to escape. Nina still looked over her shoulders multiple times before she got into and out of her oil-leaking, engine-stalling, fan-belt-breaking 2000 Ford Explorer.

Seven years and countless lap dances later, Nina was a veteran of the game. Unfortunately, she developed many of the bad habits that seem to accompany the lifestyle. Her pre-dance ritual now consisted of a shot of tequila and an occasional snort of cocaine.

On a cool autumn evening, she gave a world-class performance that would forever change her life. The recipient of this award-winning performance was a Wet Dreams regular named Larry. At least once a month he came into the club with at least ten twenty-dollar bills neatly folded and bound by a monogrammed money clip.

Unlike nearly every man, and woman, that Nina performed for, Larry never asked her for a little extracurricular activity. She wouldn't have complied anyway. Regardless of her financial needs, Nina never stooped to that low level. In the world of strippers, Larry was considered a *gentleman* because of his self-control. Compared to ninety percent of the uncouth patrons that came through the doors, Larry was a sophisticated voyeur.

Eventually, Nina got to know Larry so well that she looked forward to his visits. His proclivity to pay her more than the average customer didn't hurt either. Larry would occasionally send a bouquet of roses to the club with a note. The note was never aggressive or perverted, just a kind word and a gentle reminder that she should be careful of her surroundings.

One day, Larry called Nina at the club after he finished a business meeting and asked Nina out on a date. She usually declined these types of offers from her clients vociferously, but his offer came at a time when she desired a change. After a few seconds of holding the phone, Nina softly replied, "I'd like that. Come and get me." That one date led to a second, and two months later, they could be seen together a few times a week.

Despite Nina's rough childhood and young adult life, her sensitivity mitigated her lack of etiquette and ghetto ways. Larry was able to see past the rough exterior and latch on to the soul of a woman in need of change. He was touched when he witnessed Nina's devotion to her daughter, Precious, and her willingness to properly manage what little worldly possessions she had.

A few months after Larry foiled Big Red's brazen attempt to forcibly make Nina perform oral sex, she accompanied him to his former wife's gravesite. She held him as he cried while watching Chrissy caress her mother's tombstone. Nina's kindness on that day was all Larry needed to see. The next day, Larry decided to ask Nina to marry him.

Based on the types of guys Nina had dated since Flip's death, there was no way anyone would have predicted she and Larry would ever become a couple, let alone get married. As a matter of fact, her willingness to take the time to remember his name shocked many of her co-workers.

Larry Dennison simply did not look like Nina's type. He'd spent his entire life battling his image. At the age of forty, he stood a mere 5'7" tall and weighed 230 pounds. His hairline had started its gradual recession prior to his senior year in high school. Style was a word associated with many of his classmates, but never used in the same sentence with his name.

While growing up in San Jose, California, he was that obscure kid whom no one noticed. He was the kid that was embarrassed at the fact that he made straight A's in school. In his feeble attempt to curry favor with the popular kids in school, he deliberately sat in front of cheerleaders and jocks so that they could cheat off of his paper.

After graduating at the top of his high school class, he decided to abandon the city of San Jose and its predominantly Hispanic population, and ventured south to attend a historically black college. His goal was to connect with his culture and get as far away from the west coast as possible. His quest brought him to Dillard University in New Orleans, Louisiana.

While attending Dillard University, his social standing was further damaged by the braces on his crooked teeth and his meager wardrobe. In short, Larry was a social pariah.

Larry graduated with ease and went on to earn an MBA

and law degree from Harvard, all in relative anonymity. After completing his studies, Larry segued into the fast-paced sports arena and became a successful sports agent. By living vicariously through his clients, he was able to live out his fantasies of popularity and athleticism, all while earning a small fortune in commission.

By the time Larry turned thirty-two, he was known for his ability to sign NFL ballplayers to large contracts. But with his impeccable reputation and resume perched on the tip of his tongue, ready to be touted should an opportunity to impress presents itself, Larry still couldn't get the groupies at the parties to hold a five-minute conversation with him. If the conversation did exceed the five-minute mark, it was usually because the woman was trying to talk him into introducing her to one of his millionaire clients.

The only thing that kept Larry from drowning in his den of bachelor misery was the realization that Chrissy needed him to be strong. His obsession with being a good father enabled him to ignore the loneliness that accompanied him in bed every night. Chrissy was Larry's angel, his sole reason for living.

She was also his only connection to the happiest time in his life. When he looked into Chrissy's eyes, he saw her mother, his former wife, Deidra. She was the only woman who ever loved him unconditionally. Larry met Deidra while in college. After receiving a "B" on a statistics exam, Larry responded to a tutor ad on a school news board. It was the first and only time in his college career that he had to be tutored on any topic.

When Larry walked into the study hall and saw Deidra waiting to teach him a thing or two about statistics, he was immediately smitten with her beauty and intellect. Much to Larry's surprise, Deidra felt the same way about him.

The truth of the matter was that Larry knew that his feelings for Nina weren't as strong as the feelings he felt for Deidra. However, prior to meeting Nina, Larry felt dead and yearned to live life. Nina came along and resuscitated him emotionally. No one, especially Barbara, really understood his unwavering attraction to a woman that clearly didn't feel the same way about him.

After spending a few moments in the bathroom to clear his thoughts, Larry walked out and sat next to his sister.

"Barb, I know you mean well," Larry said as he grabbed his sister's hand. "But I need your support. Trust me on this. Chrissy and I are going to be fine."

"I want to support you, but something about this just doesn't sit well within my spirit, Larry. I give you my word that I will back your decision and not interfere, but I'm telling you right now, I'm gonna watch her like a hawk. I'm not gonna say anything, but I will be watching her. If she disrespects you or does anything to hurt my niece, I will become her worst enemy."

Larry took his finger and wiped the tear that formed in the corner of his sister's eye. He knew deep down she meant well, and because of that, he couldn't do anything but nod his head in agreement.

Together they knelt down and prayed. Barbara prayed out loud for God to bless her family and her brother's marriage. She also silently prayed that God would reveal any underlying motives Nina might have.

CHAPTER TWO

S ince their wedding day, Larry spared no expense to make his new wife and stepdaughter comfortable. He took her on a cruise to Jamaica for their honeymoon and then flew her to New York to see the stage play *The Color Purple*. When they finally returned from their honeymoon, Larry packed up his new family and moved them out to the West Coast.

Larry purchased a beautiful and spacious 5,000-square-foot home in the hills of Monterey, California. The house was equipped with a swimming pool, a whirlpool Jacuzzi, and a huge backyard.

Knowing Nina's lust for the finer things in life, Larry made sure her dream car, a 2007 black Range Rover, with its tan leather interior, and chrome twenty-inch rims, sat at the edge of the driveway, waiting to greet his new bride.

"Larry, is that what I think it is?"

"Yeah, baby, that's your dream car. I hope it has everything in it you want."

Nina screamed as she jumped out of the limousine that transported them from the airport. She jumped inside of the Range Rover wearing a smile that was so huge it gave Larry chills.

"I love it!" she screamed.

Larry chuckled as he watched his new bride climb around throughout the car and play with the buttons on the dashboard.

"Come on, sweetheart, the surprises don't end here," Larry said as he escorted Nina and their kids into the house. "Welcome to our home."

Nina looked like a first-time visitor to Las Vegas as she stood at the base of the driveway staring up at the beautiful home. Her eyes grew wider as she walked through the doorway and stared in amazement at the ceilings and floors of her new *MTV Cribs*-style home.

"Well, do you like it?" Larry asked, as he searched for some type of feedback.

"Larry, it's beautiful," Nina replied as she grabbed his face and softly kissed his lips.

"Come on, baby; I want to show you around."

Larry took his time taking Nina into every room. First, he showed her the huge kitchen with its granite counter-tops, huge center island, and stainless steel appliances. Nina was impressed, but she wasn't ecstatic about the subtle suggestion that she would be expected to cook. Nina could barely boil water, and had no intention of learning to enhance her culinary skills. She told Larry this when they got engaged, but he secretly hoped she'd change her thinking. His first wife was an awesome cook, but he would soon find out that Nina could do wonders with a credit card, but spent very little time handling pots and pans.

Larry took Nina into the huge master bedroom on the first floor. The king-size sleigh bed looked like a twin bed in the massive room. A sofa and coffee table aligned one wall and a dining table with two chairs occupied the other wall. The room was almost the size of the one-bedroom apartment Nina had just moved out of in New Orleans.

Connected to the master bedroom was the master bath. The huge bathtub was larger than her old bed and the shower with multiple showerheads looked like something out of a magazine. The walk-in closet had enough space to accommodate every piece of clothing she'd ever owned in her life. Nina was at a loss for words.

Larry took Nina and the kids upstairs and showed them the huge media room with its 60-inch plasma television mounted on the wall, pool table, and theater seating.

"You know we're going to have to host a few parties as I court prospective clients," Larry said.

"I know, that should be fun," Nina replied with excitement. She was eager to meet and mingle with Larry's celebrity associates.

The tour continued as Larry showed her the numerous bathrooms and other nooks and crannies throughout the upper floor. The balcony that lined the hallway looked down into the massive first-floor family room.

"Okay, girls, now it's time to check out your room," Larry said.

Precious started cheering and jumping with excitement as she anxiously awaited her stepfather's presentation.

Larry took them down the hall, opened the door, and smiled with pride. The shock on the faces of the women in his life was all he needed to see. Even Chrissy, who rarely showed any excitement, smiled with glee.

The room was adorned with a mural of both girls on the walls and toys galore. Positioned on each side of the room were two large queen-size beds. On one bed, there was a pillow with the name Chrissy embroidered on it and on the other bed the name Precious was embroidered on a pillow.

Precious immediately ran into the room and started playing with the life-size dollhouse. Chrissy gravitated toward the teddy bears that sat in the corner.

"The girls seem to like the room, baby; what about you?"

Nina mustered up a slight smile, but was visibly disturbed.

"What's wrong, baby?"

"Nothing's wrong. This room is beautiful, but I just figured the girls would have their own bedrooms."

"I thought about converting one of the guest rooms into Chrissy's room, but I decided not to."

"Why not?"

"I figured this would be a great opportunity for the girls to bond. They can play together and become closer. Besides, I don't like the idea of Chrissy sleeping in one of the other rooms alone because those rooms are too far down the hall. I'm accustomed to having her near me. Since you and I will be on the first floor, putting

Precious and Chrissy in the same room for a while seemed like a logical solution. After all, they're only eight years old. By the looks of it, they couldn't care less. I think they will enjoy being roommates, at least for now."

Nina didn't respond. She just stood there looking at the decorations and watched the girls play.

"Baby, what's wrong?" Larry asked again.

"I understand what you're saying, Larry, but Precious and I shared a room in that small apartment for years. I've always wanted her to have her own room so that she could have her own space. I wish you had discussed this with me before you decided to make them share a room."

Larry was clearly surprised by Nina's reaction. The issue seemed somewhat trivial to him, but he could see that it was a source of consternation for Nina.

"Okay, Nina, I hear you. I didn't mean to violate; I just didn't think it was that big of an issue. I'll call the interior decorator and have her come over on Monday and convert one of the guest rooms into a child's room."

Larry was about to ask Nina what she thought about Precious moving into one of the smaller guest rooms, so that Chrissy could be closer to the staircase. That location would make it easier for him to reach her should he need to run up and check on her. Needless to say, the question instantly became irrelevant. Before he could part his lips, Nina had already made the decision for him.

"Precious, guess what?!"

"What, Mommy?"

"This is going to be your bedroom. Larry is going to move Chrissy into one of the other rooms and this is going to be your bedroom."

"Why, Mommy? I want Chrissy to be in here with me so that we can play together," Precious replied as she looked at her mom and then glanced at her new stepsister who sat in the corner cuddling a teddy bear, totally oblivious to what was transpiring.

"You can still play with Chrissy, but this is going to be your bedroom. Remember when I told you a few weeks ago you were going to have your own room?"

"Yes."

"Well, sweetheart, now you do. This is your new bedroom in your new house. Do you like it?"

"I love it!" Precious replied, and then ran and sat next to Chrissy and started playing with the teddy bears.

Larry looked at the kids and then at his new wife. He didn't like what he'd just witnessed, but he didn't want to jump to conclusions. Nina's actions seemed somewhat self-centered and her lack of concern about how this change made him feel was bothersome. Still, he decided to chalk this up as an isolated incident. After all, she and Precious really had been living in rather cramped quarters; therefore, he could understand her desire to give Precious a room of her own.

Nina turned and looked at Larry and started talking as if the discussion about the bedroom had never happened.

"I want to go for a ride in my new car."

"Okay, let's all change clothes and we can go down to

the beach. There's a little city up the road called Seaside. We can go check out the beach over there and grab something to eat at one of the restaurants."

The view of the ocean from Highway 1 was like something out of a movie. Waves splashed against the huge boulders that lined the California coastline. Sea otters could be seen floating on their backs, basking in the sun, as families watched, laughed, and played volleyball together.

Nina wasn't accustomed to such picturesque scenery while living in the city of New Orleans. Her hometown was still trying to recover from the savage beating it took from Hurricane Katrina three years earlier. Now that she was living in California, life as she knew it had taken a permanent change for the better, and she was enjoying every moment of it.

After spending a few hours on the beach and then an hour or so at Fisherman's Wharf and the aquarium in Monterey, they were all exhausted.

Larry drove the family home. After everyone washed the day's activities off of them and put on their pajamas, it was time to tuck the girls into bed.

"It's time to get in the bed, baby. You can finish playing with your new toys tomorrow," Nina told Precious.

"Okay," Precious replied. "Mommy, can Larry come in the room to tuck me in, too?"

"Okay," Nina responded. She was a little surprised at her daughter's suggestion, but happy that Precious felt that comfortable with Larry.

"Larry, honey, come in here for a second, please."

A few moments later, Larry came into the bedroom holding Chrissy's hand.

"What's up? I was helping Chrissy brush her teeth so she can get ready for bed."

"There's a little girl here who wants you to help tuck her in," Nina said as she glanced at Precious.

"Oh really," Larry replied with a huge grin.

"Yep, so I guess you should do the honors this evening."

"I'd be glad to," Larry replied as he sat on the edge of Precious' bed. "Little Ms. Precious, I'm so happy that you are now my stepdaughter and a part of my family. I want you to know that I love you and will do all I can to make you happy."

"Thank you, Mr. Larry. I love you, too."

"First, sweetheart, I want you to stop callin' me *Mr. Larry*. I'm your stepfather now. You and I will be living together, and I don't want you to feel uncomfortable around me. I want you to feel like you can talk to me about anything. I want you to know I'm here for you."

"What do you want me to call you?"

"I don't know. What do you want to call me?"

"Can I call you Daddy?" Precious asked in the type of innocent voice that would bring even the strongest man to his knees.

Larry was caught off-guard by the question. He and Nina had never discussed the issue before. Precious had never known her real father because he had died before she could walk. A silence fell over the room. Larry looked up at Nina and noticed the apprehensive look on her face. There was a look of sadness in Nina's eyes, a clear sign of the unresolved emotions loitering in her soul.

Larry was a pretty astute businessman, but his skills were limited when it came to handling the complexities of a woman's emotions. Still, even Larry, with his minimum *game*, knew that there were certain unwritten rules that men were required to follow. As it pertains to this topic, he'd been in enough barbershops and pool halls to know that it's never cool for a man to allow another man's child to refer to him as *daddy* or *father* unless the child's biological father is deceased; he's had a heart-to-heart discussion with the biological father and the man has verbally acknowledged that he doesn't mind; or the biological father hasn't provided any emotional and/or financial support to the child.

Any barbershop psychologist, wino on the corner, or know-it-all uncle will tell you that a man who ignores this unwritten code deserves to get his ass whipped; and since receiving an ass whipping wasn't high on Larry's bucket list, Larry really would have preferred to change the topic at that moment. Unfortunately for him, the purity in Precious' eyes was more powerful than a sedative, or his fear of catching a beat down.

Larry responded, "Yes, baby girl, you can call me Daddy if you want to. Now close your eyes and go to sleep. We're going to tuck your sister in the bed now."

The smile on Precious' face was larger than the one

she had displayed when her little eyes had first witnessed the room full of toys.

"Good night," Precious said and then kissed Larry on the cheek.

"Now it's your turn, Chrissy. We're going to tuck you in," Larry said as he pried a teddy bear out of Chrissy's hand, walked her over to her bed, and helped her get underneath the covers.

"Baby, would you do the honors?" Larry asked as he turned to look at Nina.

Much to Larry's surprise and chagrin, Nina wasn't standing there. He assumed she'd stepped out for a moment to use the bathroom, so he waited and gently rubbed Chrissy's forehead. After five minutes passed, he realized Nina wasn't coming back, so he tucked his beautiful daughter in and wished her a good night's sleep.

"You are my world, Chrissy," Larry whispered into her ear. "Everything I do, I do for you. Daddy loves you and will always be here for you."

Although her handicap prevented her from verbalizing her feelings, Chrissy and Larry had developed a bond, a sort of cerebral connection. Whenever they spoke to each other at night, Chrissy would take her index finger and touch Larry's nose as a symbol of understanding.

She placed her index finger on his nose and started to smile. Larry's eyes welled as he looked at his daughter and mumbled, "Thank you, Lord, for blessing me with this child."

Once Chrissy was settled in, Larry turned off the lights and headed downstairs. As he neared the bottom of the staircase, he could hear laughter coming from the kitchen. It didn't take much deduction for Larry to conclude that Nina was on the phone talking to Val.

Larry gently crept down the stairs and positioned himself around the corner away from Nina's sight, but close enough that he could hear every word she said.

"Girl, it is off the chain! I've never seen anything as beautiful as Monterey Bay."

"Does Precious like living out there? How does she feel about the new house?"

"Precious is in love with the house, but we almost had a problem."

"What's her problem? Sounds like y'all livin' ten times better than y'all lived when you were here in this raggedy-ass city."

"I didn't have a problem with Precious; I thought I was gonna have a problem with Larry. I had to give him the look. Val, this house is huge. We have five bedrooms in here, and he had the nerve to want to make those girls share a bedroom. Now I ask you, does that make sense?"

"No, not really. Why does he want them to share a room?"

"He said he felt more comfortable with the girls sharing a room together. He didn't want Chrissy to sleep alone."

"Girl, I know you didn't like that. But, I can understand his concern. He probably wants them to sleep together so that Chrissy won't be scared. Sometimes it makes kids with autism feel more comfortable when they share a room with someone else. What was your response?"

"What do you think I said? I told him that I didn't agree. This house is too damn big to have those kids cramped into one room."

"You have a point, but the last time I checked, it was his money that bought that big-ass house."

"Val, have you forgotten who you're talking to? I'm the one with the coochie. I'm gonna get what I want. Girl, I got his ass on the coochie point system."

"Coochie what? What in the hell is the coochie point system?"

"You don't know about the coochie point system?"

"Nah, what's that?"

"It's really very simple. Every time he does something that pleases me, he gets five coochie points. It takes thirty coochie points for him to earn some of this coochie. But every time he pisses me off, I subtract five coochie points."

"So how many points does he get for buying you a new house?"

"He got about twenty points for that."

"Nina, yo ass is crazy! If he only got twenty points for buying a damn house, he's gonna have to buy you a damn palace to get fifty points!"

"Stop laughing, girl. I'm serious, that nigga is around here hustlin' for coochie points."

"Bitch, you think you slick. You doing that shit so you

don't have to have sex with that man. But, I ain't gon' lie, it sounds like that shit works. I might have to steal that and use it here on Tyrone's lazy ass."

"Damn right, it works! He's gonna get the interior decorator to come out next week and convert one of those guest rooms into a bedroom for Chrissy. My baby's a little diva; she needs her space. Girl, I'm tellin' you, never underestimate the power of the coochie point system."

At that point, Larry had heard enough. He deliberately made some noise to announce his presence before he walked into the kitchen. Nina heard him and quickly shifted the tone of her conversation.

"So, next month, you're coming?"

"If you send me the ticket, I'll be out there on the first thing smokin.' I need to get away from here for a little while."

"All right, girl; I'm going to hold you to that. Don't fake me out. Let your man know ahead of time. You can travel light because we're gonna shop 'til we drop. I love you. Talk to you soon."

Larry walked into the kitchen and opened the refrigerator. He retrieved a can of Coke from the refrigerator and then opened the top cabinet and pulled out a bottle of Jack Daniel's as Nina hung up the phone.

"Who was that?"

"That was Val. I was telling her how much we love it here. She's going to come out and stay with me for a few days when you go on your business trip."

"Oh really?"

"Yes, really. Do you have a problem with her coming out here?"

"No, I don't."

"I'm sensing some tension, Larry. What's wrong?"

Larry paused for a second before he answered. He was really trying to avoid an argument with his new bride, but he felt like he needed to set the record straight. "Actually, there is something bothering me. I feel like you disrespected me and my daughter, I mean *our* daughter, when you didn't stick around to tuck her in."

"What are you talking about?"

"I'm talking about the fact that I tucked Precious into bed, and we were supposed to both sit there and tuck Chrissy in. You walked out of the room and left us hangin.' I have a problem with that."

"Larry, my eyes were hurting, so I went into the bathroom to remove my contact lenses. When I was coming out of the bathroom, my cell phone was ringing, so I answered it. You know how Val starts talking and can't be silenced. Before I realized it, you were walking in here. Why are you trippin'?"

"Why am I trippin'?" Larry asked in a slightly raised tone. "I just feel like…you know what, don't even worry about it."

"Larry, we just got married; let's not start off on the wrong foot," Nina commented in a snide tone as she grabbed a bottle of water from the refrigerator and walked out of the kitchen.

Larry stood there for a few seconds and then gulped down the rest of his drink. *This is not starting out well*, he thought to himself.

Larry spent the next hour in his office unpacking boxes, replying to emails, and returning phone messages left by some of his spoiled clients.

One message in particular caught him off-guard. It was left by Sharrard Hogan, the projected first-round draft pick he'd recently signed on to represent in the upcoming football draft.

Wuz up, Larry! Look, man, I know you just became my agent and everything, but I need you to hook me up. My birthday is in about three weeks, playa. I need you to put together a party for a brotha. I want my shit to be off the chain. I want actors, actresses, ballplayers, pimps, hoes, and anybody else you want to invite. All I know is, my man, Jerry, is expected to be a first-round pick just like me, and his agent hooked him up last weekend. As a matter of fact, that nigga is projected to go later in the draft than me, so his shit can't be better than mine. I've been bragging to him about you, so you gotta get this shit "on and poppin," pimp! Holla at me as soon as you get this message.

Larry sat at his desk and shook his head after listening to the message. His peers had warned him that Sharrard was going to be a problem child, but he'd ignored them. The money this kid was going to command was simply too much to pass on.

Larry hated this part of his job, but if he didn't do it, some other agent would. One of the reasons he'd bought the new house and all of its accommodations was so it could serve his business purposes. It was the perfect place to throw a relatively inexpensive social gathering in a controlled environment for many of the brats he called clients.

With his business finished, he headed into his bedroom. He wasn't as annoyed as he had been an hour earlier, so he figured it would be more productive if he tried to talk to Nina now…wrong answer.

"Hey, baby, are you asleep?"

Nina had her back turned toward the bedroom entrance. She didn't answer Larry, so he assumed that she was either asleep or close to it. He couldn't see that her eyes were wide open.

"Baby, can we talk?"

Still, there was no answer from the new Mrs. Dennison. Larry sat on the edge of the bed for a moment and then stood up and took off his clothes. Although everyone else had bathed, he still hadn't. The dirt and smells from the activities of the day were still clinging to his skin. He ventured into the shower and enjoyed the drenching that ensued from the huge showerhead that hung nearly seven feet high.

With the fresh scent of Perry Ellis body lotion clinging to his body, Larry returned into the bedroom and slid his naked body under the covers. Larry's hormones were raging. He and his lovely wife hadn't had the type of sex that usually accompanies a romantic honeymoon. Nina purposely stayed drunk for most of the honeymoon to avoid intimacy. Larry was forced to settle for a hand job and three quick strokes before Nina pushed him away and passed out.

Larry never complained about the way Nina rationed the sex before they got married because his religious upbringing denounced premarital sex. However, they were married now, and he expected to be broken off on the regular.

As Larry's four-inch rock-hard penis pressed against Nina's back, he slid his hand along the side of her body. The lace undergarments she wore were enough to make a mannequin rise to the occasion. Nina's eyes opened wider. She continued to lay there as stiff as a board, purposely ignoring his gentle touch and staring at the wall adjacent to their bed.

"Baby, I'm sorry," Larry whispered. Nina said nothing. "Nina, I want to make love to you."

"Not tonight. I have a headache," Nina responded in a low dull tone.

She could feel Larry's erect penis go limp as he slowly adjusted his body. They were now lying in the dreaded back-to-back position, staring at the walls in front of them. Larry looked depressed as he contemplated the evening's events. Nina had a smirk on her face as she thought to herself: *he's going to learn that as long as I have the coochie, I run this show.*

Nina got up early to get prepared to meet Val at the airport. She made her normal trek into the bathroom to freshen up. When she walked back into her bedroom, Larry greeted her, holding a breakfast tray.

"I'm sure you're excited about seeing your girlfriend today, and the two of you are going to hang out, so I figured you'd need to start the day off with a nice breakfast. I fixed you some scrambled eggs and toast and some freshly squeezed orange juice."

Larry was expecting a warm smile and a thank you from Nina, but what he got was a nonchalant glance at the tray and a fake smile.

"Thanks. Just sit it down. I'm not that hungry. Besides, I just brushed my teeth. I might drink the juice in a few minutes. Thanks anyway."

Larry was taken aback by his wife's attitude. He placed the tray on the dresser and attempted to make small talk.

"What do you have planned today?"

"Nothing much; I'm going to pick her up and show her some of the sights. She'll probably be tired from traveling. We're going to play it by ear. I'm just excited to see her again. I'm bored out of my mind. Val will bring some entertainment here and hype things up a bit."

Nina's disinterest was obvious and made Larry's heart ache. If she opened her heart and gave him a chance, he could make her happy. He could be the kind of supportive husband that most women dreamed of having, but Nina would need to be willing to let him prove it. Unfortunately, her indifference toward him was proving to be a hurdle that even he, the master strategist, was having difficulty overcoming.

Nina walked down the steps looking like a million bucks. Her hair was perfect; her makeup was flawless; and her clothes were immaculate.

"Mommy, where are you going?" Precious asked.

"I'm going to the airport to pick up Aunt Val. I want you to behave yourself while I'm gone."

"Yes ma'am," Precious replied.

Nina scanned the room. She didn't see Larry, but she did see Chrissy sitting at the table with milk splattered all around her. Pieces of cereal were on the table, in her hair, and on her chest. It was clear the child was having a difficult time eating.

"That's disgusting," Nina mumbled and then turned and walked out.

Larry stood silently on the second floor next to the banister as he watched his wife display her contempt for his daughter.

Nina drove to the airport bumping Mary J. Blige and bobbing her head. She was extremely homesick and the thought of seeing her best friend really excited her.

Val was excited, too. She'd only left the state of Louisiana once in her entire life. Even that venture across the state line was not voluntary. It was a forced journey that was strongly urged by a mean bitch named Katrina.

Like so many New Orleanians, Val couldn't stay away from New Orleans too long. The moment she discovered that the city had been reopened after Hurricane Katrina, she was one of the first to return.

Nevertheless, Val had been waiting impatiently for this vacation and she was determined to enjoy it.

"Nina, is this your new car?" Val asked as she walked out of the airport terminal. She and Nina met at the curb and stood there hugging long enough to make pedestrians stop and stare.

"Yep, I told you Larry bought my dream car as a wedding gift."

"That's what I'm talkin' 'bout!" Val said as she tossed her small travel bag onto the backseat.

"You sure travel light."

"Hold up! You told me to travel light because we were going to shop 'til we dropped."

"And you know this!" Nina replied as she held up Larry's American Express Black Card.

"Oh shit! Is that the black card?"

"Yes it is, sweetie, and we're going to put a dent in this sucker today."

"Can I hold it, please?" Val asked as she took the card from Nina's hand and then rubbed it along her breast, belly, and pretended like she was going to slide it between her legs.

"You are crazy!"

"Girl, I didn't realize it was that thick. It doesn't feel like a regular credit card."

"That's because it ain't a regular credit card. This is a *I can get what the hell I want and there ain't no limit* credit card."

"Hello! Let's go and test that theory," Val shouted.

"But, before we start spending money, we need to stop and get some gas. My gas tank is damn near empty."

"Shiiiit, girl, my car stays on empty. I be puttin' just enough gas in there to get from my house, to work, and then back home."

"You're gonna run out of gas one day."

"I know. I hope I'm looking sexy the day that happens."

"Why?"

"Shiiiiit, I gotta look sexy because if I run outta gas, I may have to stick out my legs and hitch a ride."

"It's like that?"

"Girl, you just don't know. I might have to start selling some coochie if these gas prices go up any higher."

Nina laughed and immediately remembered why she enjoyed hanging out with Val; she was a comedian. They laughed together constantly.

"Val, your ass ain't that hard up. How much would you charge them for a half tank of gas?"

"I don't know, maybe twenty-five dollars. I'd probably

hit 'em up for fifty and a Baby Ruth if I needed to fill up my tank."

"I can see your ass hasn't changed one bit."

"Nope, I haven't."

The next fifteen minutes were spent discussing the flight and the plans for the day. Suddenly, Val remembered to ask, "Wait a minute, where's my baby girl, Precious?"

"She and Chrissy are with the live-in nanny."

"You have a live-in nanny? You have really crossed over to the white side."

"Val, I've spent the last eight years bustin' my ass, tryin' to take care of that child. I'm gonna enjoy being spoiled for the first time in my life."

"I ain't mad at cha, baby. How are you handlin' your new role as stepmother?"

"It's fine so far. I don't really have to deal with Chrissy that much; the nanny has a strong background in dealin' with children who have autism. Larry made sure of that. When she isn't around, Larry's usually there dealin' with Chrissy."

"So when are you going to dive in and 'deal' with her? You can't be married to the man and not interact with his child. Besides, based on what you've told me, Chrissy sounds like a sweet child."

"Come live with us and I'll pay you to be her personal nanny. That way you can 'deal' with her anytime you want," Nina suggested in a sarcastic tone.

"Don't tempt me; I may take you up on the offer. Did I ever tell you about my little brother that had autism?"

"You never told me you had a brother with autism."

"I don't talk about him because he died from pneumonia when he was ten years old. My mother and I really took it hard. My mom worked two jobs so I used to be his babysitter most of the time. I probably spent more time with him than she did."

"I'm sorry to hear that. I never knew."

"It's okay; I can handle it. The question is, can you handle it?"

"I don't know; it's too early to tell. I don't want to talk about that right now. Let's talk about something more interesting. What's goin' on with you and Tyrone? The last time I called you, it sounded like he was tearin' that ass up."

"Girl, he was puttin' it on me. He was givin' me my punishment."

"What?"

"He was punishin' me because I'd made him mad."

"So sex was your punishment?"

"Yeah, child; he gave me some punishment dick."

"What did you do to earn 'punishment dick?'" asked Nina with a chuckle.

"I was supposed to meet him for lunch, and I was thirty minutes late. That made him mad. But the thing that really pissed him off was the fact that it was the third time in one month I was late for lunch. Girl, he'd ordered my food because he thought I was on my way. He was sittin' there lookin' like a damn fool as he waited for me."

"What did he do when you finally arrived?"

"You gotta understand Tyrone. He has an ego that's as big as this damn car. He waited until I walked up and then told me he was leavin'. He got up and left."

"He left you sitting there?"

"He damn sure did."

"What did you do?"

"I was so embarrassed that I ate my cold food. Girl, I ain't gonna lie, I waited to try to let him cool off some before I went home."

"I gotta meet this Tyrone. He sounds like he has your ass in check."

"Whatever! Anyway, I waited as long as I could and then I went home."

"Was he yellin' when you got home?"

"Girl, he was still yellin.' I tried to argue back, but he told me to shut up."

"He told you to shut up?" Nina asked rhetorically. "What did you do?"

"What do you think I did? I shut the hell up."

"I'll be damned," Nina said.

"I know. This shit is crazy. After he put me in check, he started givin' me my punishment."

"Oh really?"

"Yeah, girlfriend. Whenever I piss him off, he punishes me with that big dick. Girl, he walked over to me and said, *'I'm gonna punish your ass.'* He grabbed me by the arm and threw me on the bed face first. The next thing I knew, he was pulling my jeans off."

"That doesn't sound like punishment; that sounds like rape."

"When you called, did I sound like someone who was protestin'? Shiiiiit—it's clear you ain't never had no punishment dick."

"I guess not," Nina replied in a regretful tone.

"It's clear you haven't. I'm tellin' you, the best time to have sex with your man is when he's pissed off with you. When Tyrone's mad, his stroke is a little faster and his dick seems to get a little longer and harder. He was even growling and shit while he was punishin' me."

"Growling?"

"Like a damn hungry wolf. He was going 'grrrrr' and telling me to apologize."

"Did you apologize?"

"Hell no, I ain't apologize! I ain't stupid. If I would've apologized, he would've stopped strokin'."

"You're a damn nympho."

"You can call me what you want; but I'm a satisfied nympho…at least in the bedroom. Nina, I can't lie. A lot of times I intentionally do stuff to make him mad."

"So you were late to lunch on purpose?"

"Girl, I was in the parking lot on the phone with my girlfriend the entire time."

Nina laughed and drove toward the Del Monte Shopping Center. She drove slowly down Del Monte Drive so that Val could see the beautiful scenery. The pristine California coast was a much prettier sight than the shores of Lake Pontchartrain that lined New Orleans.

"So what does Tyrone do for a living?"

"He doesn't do enough; that's probably my only complaint. But he's a beast in the sheets. I can't lie."

"That's all y'all have to go on, good sex?"

"Spoken like someone who ain't gettin' none. I realize your sex life is in the dumps; that's why I decided to let you listen to us that day when you called. I try to let you live vicariously through me."

"No, you're just a little freak. You were probably turned on, knowing that I was listening."

"I sure was and so were you. That's why yo ass took so long to hang up. Don't forget who you're talkin' to; I know about that little freak in you, Nina."

"Vee, it's been so long since that freak came out. I don't know if she still lives in me."

"That's because you don't have a thug like the one I got. Tyrone's been wearin' my ass out since he came home from prison."

"You'd better hope no one was wearin' his ass out while he was locked up."

"No, baby, no one has touched my man! Don't even go there," Val shouted as she rolled her eyes and neck in true ghetto fashion. "Someone sounds a little jealous."

"I *am* jealous; I can't lie. If it wasn't for my toy, I wouldn't have had an orgasm since I started dealing with Larry."

"That's a damn shame. I feel for you, girlfriend, but I can't say that I understand. Tyrone has been puttin' that *thug dick* on me."

"What do you call it?"

"You heard me. I call it that *thug dick*. Nina, he gives it to me rough, just the way I like it. You know what else he does?"

"What's that?"

"Giiiiiirl, he likes to talk shit while we have sex."

"What does he say?"

"Nina, he'll be hittin' it from the back and start askin' me kinky stuff like, *'You want me to give you three more inches of this dick?'* Girl, think about it. What would you do if your man was already pounding the coochie, and then he asks you if you wanted three more inches of dick...as if the first seven inches weren't enough?"

"The first seven inches?" Nina asked in astonishment.

"That's right, girlfriend. I said the first seven inches; you do the math. Anyway, Nina, I ain't lying. I have an orgasm every time he does that. Another thing he does while we have sex that I love is the way he eats the coochie. While he's eatin' me, he'll look up at me and say kinky stuff like, *'Umm-hmmm, I'ma eat this pussy like it's some watermelon.'*"

"Watermelon?"

"Bitch, you heard me!" Val screamed and put her arms in the air like a boxer who'd just won the title belt. "He be callin' my pussy wa-ta-me-lon! Doesn't that turn you on?"

"I'm convinced, yo ass is sho nuff crazy!"

"Whatever! He'll say sumthin' like, *I'ma stay right here until you cum for big daddy.'* But my favorite thing he says while he's eatin' me is, *'Give me my juice.'*"

"What?" Nina asked.

"Check this out. He makes me get in the doggy style position and then he'll start eatin' me from behind and smackin' my ass. Then he'll start to say, *'Give me my juice! Give me my juice!'* I'm tellin' you, Nina; I'm sleepin' with a damn porn star."

"He sounds kinky."

"Baby, he is extra kinky, and I love it! When he starts talkin' kinky to me, I lose my damn mind. I'll do anything he tells me to. There were a few times when I was out of coochie juice, and I considered puttin' on a robe and drivin' to the corner store to get him some orange juice, cranberry juice, pickle juice, pig feet juice, and any other kind of juice I could find."

Nina nearly jumped the curb as she laughed at Val. Val may have been joking, but the truth of the matter was that Nina really was living vicariously through her friend. The entire time Val described her sexual encounters, Nina sat there trying to visualize the scene, to include the size and girth of Tyrone's penis and tongue.

"So tell me, are you still rationing the coochie to Larry?"

"Unfortunately, I am. I'm so horny I had to buy a new toy."

"What do you mean, *unfortunately?* You're choosing to ration the coochie. If yo ass is horny, that's yo fault."

"I don't want to ration it, but I can't get in the mood with him. We've been married for nearly a month, and we've had sex twice. The second time we did it, I was so drunk, I barely remember what happened. I went to the sex shop last week and bought a vibrator to keep me company."

"What do you call it?"

"Excuse me?"

"What do you call your vibrator? You gotta name it. I have a name for all three of my toys."

"Val, you have three sex toys?"

"You're damn right! I would've had four by now if I didn't have to help Tyrone pay his probation officer. Child, I love my toys so much that I'm thinkin' about puttin' them in my will."

"Stop it!" Nina shouted.

"I'm serious! I don't have any kids, so I'm thinkin' about leavin' what few worldly possessions I have to my vibrators; they've earned it."

"Val, please stop; you're killin' me!"

"I'm serious. I keep 'em locked in a case inside of a cabinet in my bedroom so they won't get damaged or stolen. Nina, I'm gonna tell you somethin' I haven't told anybody."

"What?"

"You can't repeat this."

"What?"

"Nina, you can't tell anyone."

"Val, you're starting to scare me. What's wrong?"

"Nina, I mean this with all of my heart. If someone should break into my house and steal everything, I wouldn't care what they took as long as they didn't touch my vibrators. I swear; if my vibrators came up missin', I'd have to go on a manhunt."

"Girl, you scared the hell out of me!" Nina shouted and slapped Val on the arm. "I thought you were about to say something serious, and you're still talking about your damn vibrators. It's not that serious."

"Yes, it's that serious. Have you ever seen people nailing photos of lost kids on poles and hanging photos on the walls in Wal-Mart when a child is abducted?"

"Yes."

"If someone stole my vibrators, I'd start walkin' up and down the streets of New Orleans passin' out flyers and shit with pictures of my vibrators on them."

"Stop it! You're making my side hurt!" Nina screamed.

"I'm not playin'. Underneath the picture would be a caption that said, *'Have you seen this vibrator?'* My phone number would be at the bottom of the page next to a picture of me cryin'."

"What if that doesn't work?"

"I don't know what I'd do. I'd probably start a support group for women who've lost their vibrators."

"I probably shouldn't ask because you're gonna say somethin' silly, but I'ma ask anyway. What would you call the group?"

"I was thinkin' 'bout that. I don't know. I'd probably call the group somethin' like—B.B.O.D."

"What in the hell does that mean?"

"Bring Back Our Dicks! We'd even have a website called bringbackourdicks.com."

"Your ass should've been a comedian. No, I take that back; you need to see a damn psychiatrist."

"Nina, I think you're right. I take this shit seriously."

"I can see that. You said you had names for your toys."

"You're damn right! I call my little silver bullet vibrator Sneaky."

"Why?"

"Giiiiiiirl, that little thing makes my orgasms sneak up on me. I have another vibrator that's about six inches long. The tip of it kind of curves and moves around and around and the damn thing glows in the dark. When I cut off the lights, it looks like one of those swords they use to fight with in those *Star Wars* movies. I call that one Thumper because it makes me quiver."

"What about the third one?"

"Ooooh, child! Now the third one is special. It doesn't vibrate; it's just a big ass dildo. I bought that one around two years ago after Tyrone went to jail. I keep it in a special case."

"No, you don't."

"Yes, I do. When I open up that case, sparks and shit start flyin'; I swear, it's like a bright light comes shinin' out. It's like somethin' out of a movie."

"If it's that special, I'm sure it's got a crazy name."

"I call that one Meat."

"What?" Nina asked as she tried to control her laughter.

"You heard me. I call it Meat! It's about ten inches long and as thick as my wrist. Do you mind if I smoke? Girl, I need a cigarette, just thinkin' about big Meat."

"You are crazy!" Nina yelled as she wiped the tears that formed as a result of her laughter. "I can't think of any clever names."

"You have to be creative, Nina. All women name their toys. I gotta good name for yours."

"What?"

"You should call it 'Ya Boy.'"

"Ya Boy?"

"Yeah, 'Ya Boy.' Did I stutter?"

"Why?"

"You know how it is when you're talkin' to your girl-friend about your secret male friend or her secret male friend, but you don't want to say the man's name out loud. What do you usually refer to him as?"

"Ya Boy!"

"Exactly! You're not givin' poor Larry any sex. So when-ever you hook up with your vibrator, it's like sneakin' around with your secret lover."

"Okay, I'm feelin' that."

"Good! It's official. From this day forward your vibrator is officially called Ya Boy!"

While the two of them spent the entire day laughing, shopping, and sightseeing, Larry could be found at home in the kids' playroom doing fingerpainting with the girls.

Laughter could be heard coming from the room as Larry showed Precious how to cover her hand with paint and then make an imprint of her hand on the paper. He used some of the other colors to turn the imprint of her hand into a turkey. Precious looked at Larry like he was some type of god. Never in her young life had she received such undivided attention from someone other than Nina.

Even while he gave Precious the positive attention all young girls need and long for from a man, Larry never lost sight of Chrissy. As he used his right hand to point and instruct Precious on the dos and don'ts of finger-painting, he used his left hand to caress Chrissy's chin and cheeks. Larry's gentle touch was his affectionate way of letting her know that she was always in his thoughts, even when he wasn't looking directly at her.

Larry glanced at his watch and realized that he was behind schedule. He helped Precious gather her paint and supplies and put them away. With the quickness of a superhero, he picked up both girls and ushered them into the bathroom so that they could get cleaned up. He prepared a bubble bath for Chrissy and gave her a quick bath. After washing Chrissy, he took her out of the tub and carried her into the bedroom. He instructed Precious to take off her clothes and get in the tub and then went into the bedroom and got Chrissy dressed in her new pair of pajamas.

Once both girls were cleaned and looking like two little baby dolls, Larry set them up downstairs in the family room in front of the huge flat-screen television with a bowl of popcorn and two ice-cold Capri Suns. He relinquished the babysitting duties to *SpongeBob SquarePants* as he moved around the kitchen grabbing pots and skillets like a world-class chef.

When Nina and Val returned to the house, Larry was sitting down with the children preparing to eat the Mexican feast he'd cooked.

"Well, well, well, look what the wind blew in," he said as Nina and Val walked through the door.

"Aunt Val!" Precious screamed and leaped from her chair to run and give Val a hug.

"Hey, Precious! How are you doing?"

"Fine."

"Hello, Larry."

"Hello, Val. Welcome to California."

"Oh my God! This house is off the chain!"

"Well, make yourself at home...*mi casa, es su casa*," said Larry.

"Hello, Chrissy," Val said, in an attempt to be polite. Chrissy started fidgeting in her seat and making a whining sound. "I'm sorry. Did I scare her?"

"No, you didn't scare her; she always does that," Nina replied with a twinge of annoyance in her voice.

"She's just a little excited. She's fine, Val," Larry said in a defensive tone. "Would you like to eat? I made quesadillas and enchiladas. I figured the two of you might be a little hungry after tearing up the shopping malls."

"No thank you. We ate while we were out. I'm gonna

go to whatever room y'all are gonna let me sleep in while I'm here, and get ready to take a shower. I'm feelin' a little sticky."

"I understand. I had Maria, the girls' nanny, set up the guest room at the end of the hall for you."

"Thanks, Larry."

Nina gave Val an abbreviated tour of the house and then escorted her to her room.

"Nina, this house is awesome. I gotta tell you, Larry may not be the best lookin' guy I've seen, but he definitely cares about you and Precious. This man has spared no expense tryin' to make you happy."

"He has tried, I'll give him that. But sometimes money just isn't enough."

"Wait a minute. I tried to warn you on your wedding day, but you weren't tryin' to hear me."

"Yes, you did. But I can't get into him. He's just boring. I don't like the way he chews his food, always wanting to talk about politics and stuff, and he's always reading some kind of book. He's kind of nerdy to me."

"Now that you're married to him and he has you livin' large like this, you'd better learn to deal with it. I can't believe you have a problem with a man that likes to read books."

"I hear you, but I want a Tyrone to put it on me."

"Whatever! Girl, Tyrone can sling that dick, but he's broke. I'm talkin', *'Baby, give me five dollars so I can go get some cigarettes'* broke. Did I tell you what that nigga did last week?"

"No. What did he do?"

"Remember, I got that temp job as a receptionist during the daytime last month."

"Yes. He didn't come on your job and embarrass you, or any-thing like that, did he?"

"No, he didn't, but he did somethin' even more triflin.' While I was sittin' at my desk, I got a text message from him that read, *'Where is the peanut butter?'*"

"No, he didn't!"

"Yes, he did! That nigga sent me a text while I was on my job askin' me about some damn peanut butter."

"I know yo crazy ass sent a flip response."

"You know I did. I sent him a text back that said, *'Go to the store. They have a lot of peanut butter, and fill out an application while you're there.'*"

"What did he say?"

"He didn't say shit. He hasn't mentioned the words peanut butter since that day, and I refuse to buy some. To be honest, as much as I care about him and enjoy the sex, I'd rather have somebody who can *upgrade* me financially. I can be poor by myself. Nina, I'm tellin' you, if good sex is all that's missin' in your relationship, I suggest you go get 'Ya Boy' to fill in the gaps. The world is full of dick-slingin' niggas with no jobs. If your man does everything else right, I suggest you figure out a way to make that shit work."

"I hear you. Look, get ready because tomorrow we have a big day ahead of us."

"What are we going to do?"

"I told you a few weeks ago that we're going having a party this Saturday."

"Oh yeah, that's tomorrow?"

"Ahhh, hello! Tomorrow is Saturday. Pick out one of those dresses we bought today because you need to look good. There are going to be some *ballers* in here."

"Say no more. I already know what I'm going to wear."

Val was awakened the next morning by the smell of eggs, bacon, and freshly brewed coffee. The expensive sheets and soft mattress on her bed caused her to sleep like a newborn baby. The only thing that caused her to move throughout the entire night was the few times she was awakened by the sound of her own snoring.

As she stretched and tried to force her eyes to stay open, she heard a knock at the door. The giggling on the other side let her know that the tap came from the hands of a child.

"Precious, is that you?"

"Yeah," Precious replied as she let out an innocent giggle. "Mommy wants you to come eat breakfast."

"Okay, baby. Tell your mama I will be down in a second."

Val managed to shake off her sleep enough to get up and stumble to the bathroom. She quickly brushed her teeth and gargled before she grabbed her robe and trudged down the steps.

For the remainder of the day, Val acted like a teenager

getting ready for her first prom. This was going to be the kind of evening she saw the celebrities have on television.

As she put on her clothes, she peeked out of the front window to get a look at the landscaping. The property was beautiful and so were the expensive cars that lined the circular driveway. Val struggled to contain her excitement as she walked out of the room and down the stairs in search of Nina. Together they stood in the corner of the living room and checked out the sea of wealthy prospects that seem to rush into the party like the Pacific Ocean's waves.

"Nina, this party is off the chain! Girl, I've never seen this many millionaires in one room in my life."

"Val, what are you talkin' about? You've never met one millionaire in your life."

"Whatever! Your ass never knew any millionaires either before you hooked up with Mr. Money Bags, so don't try to front like you all that!"

"Whatever! I'm rollin' with them now and that's all that matters."

"Oh my God," Val mumbled as she saw a handsome, well-built man walking toward them. "Girl, that nigga is fine. Who is he?"

"His name is Sharrard Hogan. He's a football player who'll soon be filthy rich when he gets drafted. He's Larry's newest and biggest client. Larry decided to host this party in his honor."

As Sharrard walked toward Nina and Val, it was apparent that he had bad intentions. Maybe it was his exaggerated swagger or the way he licked his lips like L.L. Cool J that gave it away. One thing was for sure, he had one or maybe both of the ladies square in his sights.

"Hello, Mrs. Dennison. Who's your lovely friend?"

"This is my friend…"

"My name is Val," blurted the eager Val.

"Hello, Val, my name is…"

"You're Sharrard Hogan, the football player."

"So you know who I am?"

"Of course, I know who you are. This is a nice party."

"Yeah, it is. I owe it all to this beautiful lady's husband. My man hooked me up! By the way, Nina, where's your husband? I want to thank him again."

"I don't know where he is. I haven't seen him in an hour. He can't be too far."

"Well, if he has any sense, he won't leave you standing here alone too long. Somebody might try to scoop you up," Sharrard said in a flirtatious tone. His gaze was so piercing that it caused Nina to adjust her stance and look in the other direction.

As much as Nina tried to look away, she couldn't avoid making eye contact with Sharrard. The two of them stood there for the next five seconds eye-fucking each other. It would've lasted longer if Val hadn't put an end to it.

"Ooooh, that's my song! Sharrard, would you like to dance with me?"

"Yeah, why not," Sharrard responded, never taking his eyes off of Nina.

Val and Sharrard stood in the middle of the floor dancing closely to the latest Chris Brown tune. The sexual tension in the room was so thick it was suffocating. This was the stereotypical celebrity party, equipped with enough rated "R" behavior to fill a tabloid magazine.

White groupies were being groped in every corner as they giggled and grinned unrepentantly in the faces of the young, burly, black athletes their parents fought so hard to keep them away from. Sports agents with the persona of used car salesmen passed out business cards to anyone that would stand still long enough to listen to their sales pitches. Struggling has-been actors who could only be seen on reality television shows were talking loud and downing shots of Patrón as they basked in the most attention they'd received in years.

Still, with all the dysfunctional behavior surrounding her, Nina's eyes ignored the controlled hysteria and focused solely on Sharrard as he moved his hips from side to side. She silently marveled at his athletic physique that was on full display as his form-fitting, short-sleeved, crew neck shirt hugged his biceps. His tattooed covered forearms symbolized the defiant streak that made him insatiable to like-minded women and the guilty pleasure of even the most conservative women.

Sharrard was no dummy. He knew Nina was looking at his every move. As the song was ending, he whispered something in Val's ear. Val smiled and nodded her head in agreement. A few seconds later, the two of them left the room and went upstairs.

Nina watched closely, secretly longing to be in Val's place or maybe even join the two of them. What she didn't realize was that while she watched them, her husband was standing in a dark corner on the second floor balcony watching her. He had been sipping on a glass of wine and watching her for the past twenty minutes.

A few minutes later, Nina could see Val and Sharrard vanish as they entered and closed the door of the guest room. She looked around for Larry, but realized that finding him amongst the sea of people was going to be impossible. As she stood there fidgeting like a junkie eager to take a hit on the crack pipe, Nina contemplated whether or not to follow her best friend.

Larry watched Val and Sharrard go into the bedroom and then focused his attention back on his peculiar-acting wife.

"Mrs. Dennison, how are you?"

"Hi. Jim, right?"

"Yes, I'm Jim; Larry's coworker. This is my girlfriend, Susan."

"I'm Nina. Welcome to the party."

"Thanks for having us. Where's Larry?"

"I don't know. I haven't seen him in a while. He can't be too far. Please enjoy the party. Susan, give me your shawl, and I'll put it in a safe place."

"Thank you, Nina."

Nina took Susan's shawl so that she could take it to the empty guest room where the guests' clothing was being kept. Her offer to take the shawl had less to do with a desire to be hospitable, and more to do with having an excuse to go upstairs near Val and Sharrard.

Nina walked up the stairs at a brisk pace. She avoided looking down at the partygoers and focused on the stairs so that she wouldn't take a spill in her three-inch heels. Once she reached the top of the stairs, she turned left and started to go toward the guest room Val was in. Her momentum was stopped when someone grabbed her arm. It was Larry.

"Hey, baby, where have you been?" Larry asked.

"Oh, hey. I've been walking around mingling, tryin' to make sure everything is going as planned," Nina replied nervously.

"Where are you going?"

"I'm going to put this shawl up. It belongs to Susan, Jim's girlfriend."

"I know who she is. The guest room where the jackets are being kept is this way. Have you forgotten? You already put a few items in there," Larry said as he pointed at the guest room located in the opposite direction.

"Oh yeah, I forgot. Well, baby, you should probably go say hello to Jim. Try and have some fun. I'm gonna go and put this up."

Larry took a long sip of his wine, never taking his eyes off of Nina. He walked downstairs and started mingling with Jim and some of his other coworkers. Nina threw the shawl on the bed in the guest room and then stood in the exact same spot that Larry had stood in when he watched her. Once she was sure he wouldn't notice, she quickly walked across the hallway, which overlooked the living room, and headed toward Val's room.

Nina placed her ear against the door and tried to turn the knob. The door was locked, but the little slender key that was used to unlock the door was sitting on the top of the doorframe. Looking like a burglar trying to break into a house, she peeked over her shoulder while she reached up and grabbed the key. Her heart started to beat faster as she used the key to unlock the door.

The only thing that illuminated the room was the lamp that sat on the nightstand. The dim light created an environment that proved to be a breeding ground for lust and salacious behavior. A marijuana-induced cloud lingered lazily in the air like low-hanging storm clouds. Trying to take a deep breath proved challenging as the strawberry-scented plug-in responsible for keeping the room fresh was being bullied and rendered useless by the scent of Mary Jane that dominated the air.

Once Nina was inside the room, all she could see was Sharrard sitting on the edge of the bed staring back at her with a devilish grin. Positioned between his legs on her knees was Val, stroking and caressing his penis as she prepared to wrap her thick, sultry lips around it. Located on the bed a few inches away from Sharrard was a mirror with two and a half lines of powder cocaine.

"Come on in, baby girl," Sharrard said as he gestured for Nina to come over. "You wanna hit this weed?"

Nina stood there, speechless, with her back against the door. Val glanced over her shoulder. Her eyes seemed glazed, the look on her face was distant, and her reaction was slow and zombie-like. The residue on the tip of her nose provided evidence of where that missing half-line of cocaine now resided.

Sharrard smiled at Nina and then patted the bed, trying to entice her to come over. Nina's nipples were standing at full attention by this point. Sharrard tried to entice her once again as he winked and used his index finger to gesture for her to come over.

Nina appeared to be coming under some type of trance as she took a step toward the bed and stopped. Sharrard stood up as he witnessed his spell start to entrap another female victim. Even as he stood up, Val didn't move. Her lips were latched onto his penis so hard that a vein started to protrude from her forehead.

Sharrard noticed how Nina ignored her opportunity to leave. He took that as a sign that she wanted in on the action. To make her feel welcome, he decided to give her the show she'd obviously come in there to see.

Sharrard turned sideways so that Nina could get a better view of what he was working with. He grabbed the back of Val's head and started stroking her mouth like it was a vagina.

Nina was totally turned on by the size of Sharrard's penis and the definition in his thighs and butt cheeks. At this point, she was standing close enough to Sharrard that he was able to reach out and grab her hand. Nina didn't pull away. She didn't move any closer, but she didn't pull away. He took her index finger into his mouth and started sucking. He then took his right hand and started rubbing her breast while he sucked her finger and rammed his rock hard penis into Val's mouth.

Nina's eyes closed and opened slowly like a person on the verge of falling asleep. Her body's desire for good sex was starting to supersede her need to be cautious. She placed her hand on top of Sharrard's and guided it around her nipple. As a fire began to burn in her loins and her toes started to curl inside of her pumps, there was a knock at the door.

"Nina, are you in there?" asked the male voice.

Nina's eyes opened, and she was suddenly aware of her surroundings and the predicament she was in.

"Nah, she ain't in here," Sharrard replied.

A few seconds later, the knob on the door started to turn. Nina saw it turning and quickly stepped back and hid in the corner behind the door. She stood in that corner and held her breath like a white lady hiding from a serial killer in a poorly directed, low-budget horror movie.

Larry opened the door and stood in the doorway.

"Wuz up, dog?" Sharrard asked as he helped Val to her feet. "You wreckin' my flow."

"My bad, man. I'm lookin' for my wife."

"Well, she ain't in here, playa."

"My bad," Larry replied as he glanced at Val as she tried to look the other way, clearly embarrassed by the scene.

Larry stepped out of the doorway and closed the door. He walked back down the stairs and joined the party. Nina exhaled once the door closed. Cognizant that Larry could have been standing on the other side of the door listening, the three of them stood in the room for nearly ten seconds without making a sound.

"Well, since we're all here, we might as well get this shit on and poppin! He's gone now, baby girl; let's do this."

Nina looked at Sharrard and then at Val. Her hands started trembling and her knees started shaking. She adjusted her dress and left the room in a hurry.

No one saw Nina leave the room. Well, one person did. Maria had been standing in Precious' bedroom with the door cracked, listening to everything. She'd watched Nina go into the guest room. She'd watched Larry knock on the door looking for her. She'd heard Sharrard tell him that Nina wasn't in there and then she saw Nina run out.

Nina made it to the stairs and then looked back. Her eyes focused on Maria peeking out of the door like an eagle hovering fifty feet in the sky, zeroing in on his helpless prey. Maria slammed the bedroom door shut. Her heart fluttered as reality set in; she'd seen too much. Her days in the Dennison household were numbered and she knew it.

"Come on, Val; we have to make it to San Francisco in less than two hours," Nina screamed as she threw her makeup bag in the backseat of her truck.

"I'm comin'! I'm comin'; damn!"

"Girl, you don't understand. This is the opportunity of a life-time for Precious. This is one of the reasons I was so excited about moving to California."

"Nina, stop being so damn dramatic. This is California. If Precious doesn't make it to this audition on time, there'll be another one next weekend."

"That may be true, but I want her to make it to this one. I love Old Navy clothing. Not only is this a nationwide campaign, but the children that are chosen get a year's supply of clothes."

Val didn't bother to respond. She stared out of the window at the ocean as they rode north on Highway 1. The sight of the ocean waves and the hang gliders hovering over the Pacific Ocean had her awestruck.

As they skirted past Santa Cruz and onto Highway 17 where the road cuts through the mountainside, Val started to compare the beautiful landscaping to what she'd grown accustomed to in New Orleans. She pondered her life and the stagnation that awaited her upon her return.

With each passing second, Val's mood started to reflect the growing resentment she was feeling toward Nina's new standard of living. Nina had a millionaire husband, while she was stuck with Tyrone and his long dick, but short finances. Soon her thoughts drifted toward her sexual encounter with the new multi-millionaire Sharrard Hogan.

"Has Larry said anything about Sharrard?"

"Like what?"

"I don't know, anything."

"He hasn't said anything about him since Sharrard signed his contract last weekend. Girl, Larry got him a five-year contract worth thirty million dollars. He got ten million of that in a signing bonus."

"Ummm…that's nice."

"It damn sure is, and I can see your eyes twinkling over there. Have you heard from Sharrard since the party? I know y'all didn't talk much that night because you had your mouth full," Nina said with a chuckle.

"Aww, bitch, stop frontin'. If your man had knocked on that door a few seconds later, he would've seen you pushing me off Sharrard's dick so you could have a turn."

"Val, watch your damn mouth! Precious can hear you."

"No, she can't. She's asleep."

The two of them sat quietly for the next five minutes.

Val's temperature was coming to a boil as she thought about the life she could have with Sharrard, and then compared it to her current life back in New Orleans with Tyrone. Eventually her curiosity got the best of her, so she asked once again about Sharrard's contract.

"How much was Larry's cut?" Val asked.

"Larry's cut of what?"

"Sharrard's contract!"

"He didn't tell me, but I've been on the Internet doing some research. Larry's fee was somewhere in the ballpark of one million dollars after the firm got its cut and after taxes."

"Damn! I didn't know Larry was ballin' like that."

"Yeah, child, we're ballin' like that. Sharrard is his biggest client, but he ain't Larry's only client. He's been quiet about his exact net worth, but he's worth a few million. He even invested in some of those new Vitamin Water drinks. I've been playin' it cool, but I'm going start snooping harder in a few months. I'm tryin' to wait until we've been married for a little while. What's his is mine."

"I ain't tryin' to get too far into your business, but did he make you sign a prenup?"

"Yes, you are tryin' to get in my business, but that's all right, you my girl. Yes, he did make me sign a prenup."

"Why did you sign it? As much as that nigga was sweatin' you, he would've married you with or without a prenup. I wouldn't have signed it."

"The prenup I signed doesn't give me any child support;

after all, Precious isn't his biological daughter, and I didn't feel right about stickin' him up for money based on that. But it guarantees me a hundred thousand in cash if our marriage lasts at least one year and two hundred fifty thousand in cash if we last at least two years."

"That ain't shit if he's worth as much money as you said! What if y'all last more than two years?"

Nina smiled and looked at Val. "If we last more than two years, he has to tear up the prenup, and I get half of everything he owns."

"Bullshit!"

"I ain't lying. He even put it in writing in the contract. Trust me, since he got all that money for Sharrard, his phone has been ringing off the hook. It seems like every free agent in the league is tryin' to get Larry to be their agent. That means that in two years, his net worth is going to be double what it is now."

"That nigga might have some book smarts, but he ain't got an ounce of game," Val concluded.

"Why do you say that? You just said that you wouldn't sign a prenup, so apparently you don't agree with them anyway."

"Oh, don't get it twisted; anyone with a lot to lose should have a prenup drawn up to protect their money. If I had a lot of money I would get one, but that doesn't mean I would ever sign one if somebody gave it to me."

"Now you understand why I have to play my cards right for the time being."

Val rolled her eyes in disgust at Nina. She'd been hangin' out with Nina in California for a little more than two weeks, and was beginning to grow tired of Nina's constant bragging. Val knew that Nina was enjoying flaunting her good fortune.

Val and Nina were good friends, but there was always a competitive undercurrent between them. When they were both strippers Nina would get more aggressive on stage and during lap dances if she noticed that Val had earned more money. When local rappers asked Val to be in their videos, Nina deliberately showed up on the set looking sexier to steal the attention.

Trying to compete with Nina's bank account was futile so Val conceded this round of sparring, but she was determined to win the next.

Val took a glance at Precious and Chrissy in the backseat and then smirked before she commented, "You mean, what's his is yours and Chrissy's."

Nina sat there, silent. She tried to pretend she didn't hear Val's comments, but the frown lines that streaked across her forehead like lightning across the sky were a clear giveaway that Val had struck a nerve.

"Yep, you know Larry's going to take care of baby girl back there in the backseat before he takes care of anyone," Val replied and then looked over the headrest and waved at Chrissy.

Chrissy was totally oblivious to the innuendo that had spewed from Val's mouth and bounced around the car like a rubber ball, occasionally popping Nina upside the head.

"By the way, why is Chrissy with us? Why didn't you leave her with Maria? As a matter of fact, where is Maria? I haven't seen her around the house in a few days."

"You haven't seen her because I sent her home for the weekend," Nina barked.

"Why'd you send home?"

"I sent her home because I'm going to fire her ass next week."

"I thought you liked Maria?"

"She's starting to get sloppy. We pay her good money to take care of Chrissy and she isn't doing enough to earn it."

"What did Larry have to say?"

"He doesn't know."

"Ouch. Don't you think you should tell him that you're going to fire the woman he handpicked to watch his handicapped daughter?"

"Val, I don't need you tell me how to run my household!"

"Excuse the hell out of me," Val replied in a flippant tone. "I'm gonna make sure I got a lot of popcorn because I'm gonna get a kick out of watching you try to take care of that child until you hire a new nanny."

Nina was silent for a few moments. She tried to focus as she crossed three lanes trying to get off Highway 17 and onto Highway 101 heading toward San Francisco. It didn't take long for Nina to learn that aggression can be an asset on the fast-paced California highways.

The skies turned dark and storm clouds swooped in

from over the ocean as the ladies sped toward their destination. It didn't rain often in this part of California, but when it did rain, it usually came hard and swift.

"I haven't started looking for a new nanny yet."

"Why not? You need to look for one or get prepared to have some long days ahead."

"Actually, I'm kind of glad you brought that up. Do you remember our discussion when I first picked you up from the airport?"

"What discussion?"

"You and I talked about you coming here to be a nanny for us. You said you had experience with autistic children."

"Nina, stop trippin'!"

"I'm not trippin.' I know you are tired of dancing in that sleazy ass strip club."

"Oh, now it's sleazy? You weren't sayin' that shit when you were making your ass clap on that pole."

"Whatever. All I'm saying is that you can live here with us for free, and we will pay you more money than you're earning now."

Val pondered the proposition. The more she thought about it, the more intriguing the offer sounded. Nina could see she had Val's mental wheels turning so she decided to sweeten the pot to seal the deal.

"I doubt you'll be working for us very long."

"Why do you say that?"

"Girl, with your looks and that body, you'll probably hook up with one of Larry's millionaire friends within the first two or three months. The next thing you know, you'll be giving parties and shit at your own mansion."

The glossy look in Val's eyes told Nina all she needed to know; the thought of wealth had Val hooked.

"What about Larry?"

"What about him! Girl, he'll be home in two days; I'll make sure I give him a little coochie before I tell him. Trust me, after I whip it on him, he'll agree to do whatever I tell him to."

"We'll see," Val replied in a dry tone.

"Is it a deal?"

"More money than you're payin' Maria?"

"Yep!"

"Are you gonna help me land Mr. Sharrard Hogan?"

"I'll arrange another dinner party to get the two of you to- gether again."

"Then we've got a deal."

"My girl!" Nina said with a huge conquering smile.

The auditions were being held in a slender three-story loft house nestled on the corner of Lombard and Van Ness in the heart of San Francisco. Nina had only been in that area of the city once so she was struggling to identify the landmarks.

The front of the loft looked like all of the other homes that seemed to fit together like Lego blocks along the steep San Francisco streets. If it weren't for the line that snaked from the entrance, down the street, and then around the corner, there would have been no way of knowing where the auditions were being held.

"Are there any black people in San Francisco?" Val asked sarcastically.

"What? Of course there are black folk here."

"I'm serious. I haven't seen a black person yet. All I see around here are Asians and white folk walking these big-ass dogs."

"Yeah, they do like their dogs out here in California. These people treat their dogs better than they treat other humans."

"They all look dirty."

"What?"

"These white folk, they all got this grunge look about 'em."

"Girl, that's their style out here. That's one of the first things I noticed when we moved. Where we're from, black folk get dressed up to go to the corner store. But these white folk out here don't care about all that. All they do is walk their dogs, ride their bikes, jog all over the damn place, drink Starbucks coffee, and spend the trust funds their parents left for them."

"Shit, I'm lookin' in the wrong direction," said Val. "I need to try to catch me one of these white boys with a trust fund. If he doesn't have a trust fund, he may at least have a six-figure income."

"What would you do with a man with a six-figure income?"

"I'd cook for him every day and let him get some of

this sweet ass whenever he wanted it. Girl, I can't even lie; at this point, I'll just take a man with a five-figure income."

"What would you do with a man who had a seven-figure income?" Nina asked, her subtle way of bragging about her husband's income.

"Girl, please! If I had a man with a seven-figure income, I'd let him fuck me in the ear."

"Yo ass is crazy!"

"Shiiiit! You can call me crazy all you want, but I'd keep a tube of KY Jelly next to my ear and be ready to use it if that nigga bringin' home seven figures."

"What the…" Nina blurted out as they pulled up to the audition site and she saw the long line outside.

"Girl, it is two o'clock and you'd be lucky if Precious gets to audition before five."

"Bullshit!" Nina said with much attitude.

She parked the car, grabbed her makeup kit, and snatched Precious out of the seat. Val hopped out of the car and closed the door.

"Do you have to slam my damn door like that?!" Nina shouted.

"My bad, Nina, damn!" Val replied as she rolled her eyes at Nina. "Wait a second. I'm tryin' to get Chrissy together."

"Girl, I ain't got time to wait on you and Chrissy's slow asses. I gotta get my baby to the front of this long-ass line!"

Nina didn't bother to look in Val's direction as she spoke. She gripped Precious' tiny hand and walked toward the front of the line with an angry expression plastered on her face. She looked as mad as a black woman who'd just found out her husband had left her for a white woman.

The looks she received from the other mothers were deadly, but they didn't deter Nina from marching to the front of the line and approaching a thin-framed Hispanic male.

"My name is Nina Dennison. My husband is Larry Dennison, the sports agent. Jeremy told my husband to bring our little girl here at two o'clock today. Well, it's two o'clock and I'm not about to stand out here for two or three hours. Where is Jeremy?"

"Actually, he has been waiting for you, Mrs. Dennison. Follow me."

Nina smiled and gave a snooty look to the mother who stood at the front of the line. The woman was not shy about protesting Nina's bully tactic.

"Right over here, Mrs. Dennison. Jeremy, this is Larry Dennison's wife, Nina, and their daughter, Precious. They're here to audition for the lead part."

"Hi, Nina," Jeremy said. "Larry and I know many of the same people. Please forgive me for rushing, but as you can see, we have a lot of people to see today."

"I understand. I'm just happy that…"

"Yes, yes. Young lady, I'm going to need you to take that child and stand over there," he instructed Val in a rude tone.

Val grabbed Chrissy by the hand and stood off to the side.

"Now, Nina, I need you to stand here out of the way.

My assistant is going to spend a few seconds giving… what's the child's name?"

"Precious."

"Yes, Precious, interesting ethnic name."

"No, he didn't!" Val shouted from across the room.

"Quiet on the set, please!" Jeremy shouted as he rolled his eyes at Val. "Now, Precious, I need you to stand over there next to the wall and look into the camera and say the lines. Do you know the lines?"

"Yes."

"Good. Start saying your lines whenever you're ready."

"Okay," Precious replied, clearly nervous. "My mommy took me to…"

Precious was interrupted by a whining sound; it was Chrissy.

"Excuse me. Lady, could you please quiet that child?" Jeremy said to Val.

Val rolled her eyes at the obnoxious director and started whispering into Chrissy's ear. A few seconds later, Chrissy seemed to calm down.

"Thank you! Now, Precious, I want you to try again."

"My mommy took me to Old…"

The whining sound started again. This time Nina marched over to Chrissy, grabbed her by the arm, and said, "Chrissy, calm down!"

"Nina, you ain't helpin' the situation by grabbing this child that way. You're only goin' to upset her."

"Well, you're supposed to be the expert on handling autistic kids. Do your damn job, Nanny!"

"You gonna make me curse your ass out in here," Val said in a low tone.

"Can we please get started?!" shouted Jeremy.

"I'm sorry, Jeremy. This is my stepdaughter and she's autistic. Sometimes she makes these sounds when she gets nervous."

"Well, honey, I'm on a tight schedule, so I need you to figure out a way to keep her quiet, or I'm gonna move on to the next child."

Nina turned to Val and mumbled, "Val, I don't care what you have to do to keep her quiet, but you need to figure out a way. Take her little retarded ass outside if you have to."

The excitement of the moment must have rattled Chrissy because she started screaming uncontrollably.

"That's it!" Jeremy shouted. "Mrs. Dennison, I don't have time for this."

"Wait, Jeremy; my friend is gonna take her outside."

"It's too late, honey! Next child, please!"

Nina had mastered the wealthy, spoiled housewife routine. Although she'd only been married for a short time, she'd already grown accustomed to pouting and getting what she wanted. But she had no control of this situation. Jeremy had all of the control and to make matters worse, he was an even bigger diva than she was.

As Nina, Val, and the kids left the audition, the protesting mother whom she skipped earlier walked past with a smirk.

"Maybe next time," the woman commented.

Nina gave the woman the one-finger salute and exited the building. As she walked briskly to her car with Precious struggling to keep up, she thought to herself, *This is the last time I let Chrissy ruin something for my baby.*

CHAPTER THREE

T he weather was starting to change quickly. The children were asleep in their seats, and Val was struggling to keep her eyes open. She allowed her head to rest against the window as she drifted in and out of sleep.

The silence created a perfect environment for Nina's anger to grow. She glanced back at Chrissy four times within the first hour of the drive. A part of her wanted to give the child a smack across the head. Val's eyes opened long enough to notice her friend's vicious glare.

"Nina, that's a child. She can't help her condition."

"Val, I don't want to hear that shit!"

"I don't care what you feel like hearin', you don't need to take your frustration out on that child. We will be back at the house in a few minutes. I suggest you go inside and get a drink of wine to help calm your damn nerves."

"I don't know if I can deal with this."

"You have no choice but to deal with this; she comes as a part of a package deal. The last time I checked, if it wasn't for her daddy, Precious wouldn't be attending any auditions."

The rumbling of storm clouds interrupted their conversation. The dark, menacing clouds wasted no time dumping gallons of water onto the landscape. This torrential downpour made it difficult for Nina to see.

As they blew through Pacific Grove and into the city of Monterey, Nina pondered her next move. She had to come up with something that would make her desire to get rid of Maria an easy sell to Larry.

As she maneuvered her SUV along the winding road that led to their gated community, the lake that ran alongside the road looked like a black canvas. The two-lane road they traveled was smothered in the darkness brought on by the setting sun and dirty brown-colored rain clouds.

"Val, I have some decisions to make."

"Nina, stop being overly dramatic. There'll be other auditions. I'll stay at home and watch Chrissy the next time, and you can take Precious by yourself."

She turned and looked at Val, and then looked out the front windshield again. With her eyes squinted and a firm grip of the steering wheel, Nina attempted to brave the elements.

A few landmarks alerted Nina that her home was less than five minutes away. As she struggled to see through the wall of rain outside of her window, Nina envisioned pouring a glass of wine, sinking into a nice hot bubble bath, and then retreating to her bedroom.

Suddenly, her daydream was interrupted by a set of bright dots that appeared to be suspended in midair.

The dangling dots appeared to get closer and closer; so close that Nina soon realized the dots were actually headlights that belonged to an oncoming SUV.

Nina jerked the steering wheel to the right in a desperate attempt to avoid the vehicle. Unfortunately, the response of her high-priced vehicle was too good. The car maneuvered so well that her reflexes weren't fast enough to readjust before she crashed through the frail wooden railing that stood between the road and the edge of the cliff.

The tree that protruded from the lake's surface was probably one hundred years old. Its branches were massive and spawned smaller, curvy branches that were the width of a toddler's arm. Only an inanimate object such as this could ignore the urge to flinch as Nina's 2007 Range Rover hurled through the rain-filled sky and landed on top of it.

The screams that filled the air were silenced instantly as the huge branch shattered the front windshield, cut into the deployed driver's side airbag like a hot knife through butter, and pierced Nina's right shoulder. Val was knocked partially unconscious by the force of the crash. Blood streamed from her scalp and along the bridge of her nose, as she slouched in the front passenger seat like a blood-soaked ragdoll. The right side of the vehicle was partially submerged as the left side relied heavily on the tree branch to keep it propped above the water. The rain seemed to relish this carnage as it came down harder, seemingly out of spite.

As the creaking sound of metal subsided, the only thing that could be heard were the soft moans of a child—make that two children. Precious was positioned in the passenger seat directly behind her mother. Like Nina, she was benefiting from the position of the tree branch. Her right foot was the only part of her body that touched the surge of water that was starting to fill the vehicle.

Chrissy wasn't as lucky. Much like Val who struggled in the front passenger seat, being positioned on the right side of the vehicle brought her one step closer to death. With her face partially submerged, Chrissy was able to manage a moan. Precious joined in as the sounds from the two children served as the only indication of life inside the demolished vehicle.

"Mommy!" Precious called out in a barely audible tone. "Help me, Mommy!"

"Uhh, uhh," Chrissy moaned. Her limited speech capabilities combined with injuries from the crash made it impossible for her to utter anything else. Nina's maternal instincts must have kicked in because she awakened from her unconscious state at the sound of her daughter's cries for help.

"Precious!" Nina screamed as she twisted and moved around in her seat. "Mama's here, Precious! Mama's right here!"

"Help! Help me, Mommy!"

"Val, are you okay?" Nina asked.

Val didn't reply. Truth be told, Nina didn't wait for a reply. She used her right hand to release the seatbelt and her left hand to push the tree branch more toward Val. At that moment, Nina had one thing on her mind; getting to Precious.

When Val finally regained consciousness, she realized the severity of their situation. "Nina, I think my arm is broken. Grab Chrissy, the car is sinking on this side," she mumbled.

Nina didn't respond to Val, but she did scream as she maneuvered her body so she could look over her seat to see her child. The tree branch had taken a hunk of flesh from Nina's right shoulder, and she was in excruciating pain.

"Nina, grab Chrissy; she's going to drown!" Val shouted a second time as water started to invade her mouth and nostrils.

Nina watched Chrissy as she struggled to keep her head above water. Nina's gaze was interrupted by the sound of Precious' voice.

"Mommy, help me!" Precious screamed. "I'm scared, Mommy! Help me!"

"I see you, baby! Mommy's coming!"

"Nina, the branch is in my way. I can't reach Chrissy; grab her before she drowns."

"Okay," Nina replied, as she started to push the branch out of her way so that she could get a better angle at Chrissy.

The force from her push was all the branch could take. The snap of the branch sounded like a firecracker exploding in a closed closet. The entire rear end of the vehicle dipped and the front portion went up like a seesaw. Nina was nearly thrown over her seat and into the water when the car shifted. Val was the biggest beneficiary of this event because her head and shoulders were now elevated above the water.

"Lord, please help us," Val prayed aloud.

Nina screamed as she witnessed the girls' heads slowly disappear beneath the surface of the water that now dominated the car. Val looked helpless as her severely broken arm prevented her from helping.

"Precious!" Nina screamed.

As if on cue, a tiny arm emerged from the water. The attached hand wiggled while the stretched fingers desperately searched for something or someone to hold on to.

"Nina, look, it's Chrissy's hand! Grab her, Nina; she's alive!"

Nina looked at Chrissy's outstretched hand. She wanted to grab the child's hand and pluck her from the water, but all she could think about was saving Precious.

"Hold your breath, Precious!" Nina screamed. "I gotta save my baby!"

"Nina, grab Chrissy's hand!"

Nina climbed over the seat and reached along the side of the seat Precious sat in and released the seatbelt. Fortunately, Precious had developed into a pretty good swimmer for her age. Nina's insistence that Precious take swimming lessons as early as the age of five paid off. The moment Precious went underwater, she started holding her breath the way her swimming instructor taught her.

With her child cradled in her arms, Nina managed to open the passenger door. Like two rubber ducks bobbing up and down in a bathtub, she and Precious appeared, disappeared, and then reappeared in the water. On the other side of the car, a splash could be heard. Suddenly, a light shone brightly on Nina and Precious. From the shore, silhouettes could be seen pointing and moving toward them.

"I got one!" shouted a man.

"I got two!" shouted another man as he dragged Nina and Precious toward the shore.

Nina and Precious were gasping for air as they sat on the shore surrounded by unfamiliar faces. Val's voice could be heard as two women attempted to apply a makeshift splint to her compound fractured arm.

"Get Chrissy!" Val screamed.

"What is she saying?" asked a rescuer.

"Chrissy is in the backseat!" Val blurted out.

"Oh my God! She said someone was in the backseat."

As the car became totally submerged, a half dozen bystanders dove into the water and swam toward the old tree that once cradled the Range Rover. Seconds turned into minutes as the swimmers risked their lives to reach the car. Within minutes, five of the would-be rescuers returned gasping for breath and looking dejected. The last diver seemed to be lost in the unforgiving water like the vehicle.

"Honey!" screamed the wife of the final rescuer.

As he appeared from the murky water carrying a small lifeless body, the man's tears were disguised by the dirty lake water that saturated his face. He placed the lifeless body on the ground and attempted CPR, but after three minutes of failed resuscitation, he gave up. No one had to ask whether there was still a chance to save the child's life. The look on the rescuer's face and the child's limp limbs said it all; Chrissy was dead.

Val put her head down and cried, "No, no, Lord, not Chrissy. She's only a child!"

Nina sat a few feet away, holding Precious, as she watched a total stranger carry her now deceased step-daughter to the shore. She grabbed the back of Precious' head and pressed her face up against her chest and breast so that the child didn't have to witness the horrible scene. The emotion and drama that filled the air was suddenly replaced with a chilling silence.

As if on cue, every head bowed as Chrissy's body was placed on the ground; every head but Val's. Val's anguish and tears were on full display as she planted a gaze on Nina that was so steely it would have scared Satan.

Larry was on his way to the airport when he got the phone call from Nina informing him of the car accident. Nina didn't tell him that Chrissy had died because she feared he would be too devastated and have no one around to help console him. Her assumption was correct.

Being forced to wait until he returned to town to learn all of the details didn't change his reaction. Larry was an emotional wreck as he wondered what happened to his family, especially Chrissy.

When he burst through the emergency room doors, he looked as if he had been in a car wreck. His tie was loosened around his neck. The top buttons on his expensive French cuff shirt were unfastened and perspiration beads covered his brow, cheeks, and neck.

"Where is my baby?"

Val stood up to greet Larry as he entered.

"Larry, I need to talk to you."

"Are you okay?" he asked. "Where is Nina? How is Precious? Where is Chrissy?"

"I'm fine. Precious is still real rattled by what happened. Nina is in the back talking to the doctor."

"Where is Chrissy? Is she okay? I want to see my child."

"Larry, calm down."

At that moment, Nina came from the triage area. She looked into Larry's eyes and started to cry.

"Nina, where is Chrissy?"

Nina didn't answer. She lowered her head and walked away. Larry instantly knew that something was wrong. He barged into the triage area and started calling Chrissy's name.

"Nurse, I'm looking for my daughter, Chrissy; I mean, Christine Dennison."

"Mr. Dennison, I need you to step into this room."

"I want to see my damn daughter!"

"Mr. Dennison, please step into the room so that we can talk."

The E.R. physician on duty accompanied Larry and the charge nurse into the small office.

"Mr. Dennison, I'm sorry to inform you that your daughter didn't survive the crash. She drowned. She was trapped in the backseat of your wife's SUV. I'm very sorry for your loss."

Larry stood there in shock. He didn't move an inch as the doctor tried to ask him if he was okay. The hospital's chaplain walked into the room and introduced himself. Larry could see the chaplain's lips moving, but he didn't hear a word the man said. Images of Chrissy's lovely face were the only thing on his mind.

Nina and Val sat in the lobby, wondering what was happening.

"Nina, don't you think you should go in there and check on your husband?" Val asked.

Nina sat there like a statue.

"Nina!" Val shouted.

Nina finally looked at Val.

"You need to go and check on your husband!"

Nina finally nodded her head in agreement. "I'll be back. If the doctor comes out, make sure you get an update on Precious for me."

As Nina stood up, she heard a heart-wrenching scream; a scream that would be embedded in her psyche for the remainder of her life. Reality had sunk in and had shaken Larry to his core.

When Nina entered the small office she saw her husband on his knees sobbing uncontrollably. That same heartfelt cry that had been lying dormant inside of Larry's diaphragm since Deidra's death eight years earlier had resurfaced.

Nina walked over and kneeled next to him. It was the first public display of affection she'd ever shared with Larry. Larry's body seemed to shrivel as he went from his knees and curled up into the fetal position. His pain reverberated throughout the emergency room. Larry's unrestrained pain was so moving that it caused otherwise callous and aloof nurses to seek out the nearest Kleenex box.

Nina sat there in the middle of the floor with him. She looked on helplessly as she pondered her contribution to his mourning.

Chrissy's funeral was attended by many of Larry's co-workers and clients. There wasn't a dry eye in the house as Larry struggled to control his emotions.

Anyone who knew anything about Larry's personal life recognized the bond between him and his daughter. He'd never hidden his devotion to Chrissy. That characteristic alone was enough to overshadow his intellect and command respect from the people he associated with.

Nina sat next to Larry and held his hand throughout the entire funeral. Although she had never taken the time to connect to her now deceased stepdaughter, she also felt the despair of the moment.

Val sat on the pew behind Nina and Larry. Her broken arm was in a cast and secured to the side of her body with a black sling. She looked uncomfortable, like she didn't want to be there. Sitting to her immediate right was a caramel-complexioned, curly-haired black man with a clean-shaven face and a huge scar that ran from his left earlobe to the corner of his mouth. The mysterious man was Val's boyfriend, Tyrone. The scar that he wore like a badge of honor was one of his mementos from prison.

Nina had heard a lot about Tyrone, but had never actually met him. She glanced over her shoulder when she heard Val sobbing, and could feel the intensity of Tyrone's stare. His stare seemed inappropriate considering the events of the moment, and the smirk he hit her with when their eyes met seemed downright creepy.

As the nearly two hundred attendees exited the funeral, Larry tried to appear strong so that he could receive everyone's condolences and thank his supporters for coming, but the weight of the heartache he felt made it difficult for him to stand, literally.

As Barbara escorted her younger brother to the limousine, Nina did her best to hold down the fort. She shook dozens of hands, but received the cold shoulder from Val as she walked past. Tyrone, on the other hand, made it a point to stop and express his sorrow to Nina.

"Nina, we've never formally met, but I'm Tyrone, Val's friend."

"Hello, Tyrone. Thanks for coming."

"No problem; I wanted to pay my respects. This was a tragic event. You must really be feelin' the pressure."

"What do you mean?"

"I'm talkin' about the pressure you must feel tryin' to keep Larry from finding out what really happened during the crash."

"Excuse me?"

"Val told me how you watched poor little Chrissy drown. Don't worry, your secret is safe with me…for now," Tyrone replied and then whispered into Nina's ear. "It would be a shame if Larry found out that you had a chance to save his little helpless handicapped daughter, but opted to let her drown."

Nina looked as if she'd seen a ghost. Her heart rate sped up significantly and her eyes immediately filled with water. Her body trembled as she looked deeply into Tyrone's wicked eyes.

"Val told you that?" she asked.

Val stood a few feet away, leaning against a tree. She stared at Nina the same way she had done the night of the crash. The hatred in her eyes could be seen from afar.

"We'll be in touch," Tyrone said and then gave Nina a soft pinch on her side. "Trust me, sweetheart; I'll definitely be seein' yo fine ass again."

As he walked away, he turned around and attempted to give Nina a piece of paper.

"Here's my phone number. Call if you need anything."

Nina turned and walked away. Tyrone was noticeably embarrassed. So he turned to Maria, who was standing a few feet away.

"It's obvious she's upset. You're the nanny, right?"

Maria nodded. "Yes."

"Good. Please give Nina this phone number later on. I want to be there for her and the family, in case they need something."

Maria took the wrinkled piece of paper with Tyrone's cell phone number scribbled on it.

Nina's chilling encounter with Tyrone forced her to remember the traumatic crash all over again. Within seconds, she replayed in her mind every moment inside of the SUV: the terrifying screams; Val's voice urging her to save Chrissy; Precious calling her name; Chrissy's hand disappearing beneath the surface of the water. Her memory of the accident was distressingly clear.

Nina's tense moment was interrupted by the tug on her dress by her daughter.

"Mommy, I want to go home."

"Okay, baby. We're going home in a few minutes."

The mood at the Dennison household was much like you would expect after a loss as tragic as this. A few of the family's closest friends and relatives were congregating in the living room. Barbara was in the kitchen fixing a pot of coffee and trying her best to maintain control of the somber environment.

Nina gave Precious a snack and then took the child to her bedroom.

"Sweetheart, I want you to play with your toys for awhile. Mommy is going to go and talk to Daddy."

"Can I come?"

"No, baby, I have to talk to Daddy alone. When I'm finished, I'll come back in here and talk to you."

Nina exited the room and then walked downstairs toward her bedroom where she knew she'd find her husband. Larry was sitting in the lounge chair located in the far corner of the room. He held a picture of Chrissy in one hand and her favorite teddy bear in the other. It was the same teddy bear she'd gravitated toward the first day he'd brought them to their new house.

"Do you feel like talking?" Nina asked, not really sure what else to say.

Larry stared at the picture. Tears rolled down his face as he strengthened his grip on the teddy bear. "Tell me what happened to my baby."

"Larry, I told you what happened."

"Tell me again."

Nina paused for a moment. Deep down she knew that she should probably tell Larry that she had a decision to make and she chose to save her own child. But there's no way he'd understand her choice. How could he? The odds had been stacked against Chrissy since her birth.

The odds had become more stacked against her when they were all trapped in that car. At that moment, she needed more help than ever before and her request for assistance was ignored. Nina felt that her decision to save her own child was no different than that of any mother placed in the same position. Still, the odds of her grief-stricken husband understanding and sympathizing with the quagmire she faced were minuscule at best.

"We were driving down the road that leads to this community. It was raining real hard, and I was having difficulty seeing the road. Suddenly, a car appeared, and I swerved to avoid hitting it. The car spun out of control and went through the barrier. We landed in the lake on top of a tree that stuck out of the water.

"I was knocked unconscious for a moment, I'm not sure how long. Val's arm was broken, and the girls were in the backseat moaning and crying. I was trying to climb into the backseat to get the girls, but I was trapped by a branch that came through the front windshield. That's how I hurt my arm."

Nina paused for a moment to gauge Larry's mood. He stared at her intently, seemingly hanging on her every word. Nina swallowed the little spit that remained in her parched mouth and continued.

"The truck started to sink into the water, and we were all starting to drown. I was able to open my door. Precious was sitting behind me, and she was able to get out of her seat. I think her ability to swim helped her. Before I knew it, she was in my arms. Chrissy and Val were on the other side of the car. I tried to grab Chrissy but, all of a sudden, I felt myself being pulled away. When I finally got pulled to shore by the man who saved us, I looked up and saw another man dragging Val to the shore. The last man that came out of the water was carrying Chrissy. She seemed a little limp, but I couldn't tell if she was alive."

"She looked limp?"

"Yeah, her body looked a little limp. There were people all around. Things were happening fast."

"There's something you said that has me confused. How did Precious get out of the car and end up in your arms? I saw the truck. The rear passenger door was smashed badly; how did she get out?"

Nina was stumped. She'd practiced her story to the point that it sounded more like an alibi. She could recite her version of what happened in her sleep, but Larry's question was unexpected and left her searching for a response.

Nina could see that Larry's question wasn't rhetorical. He expected an answer. She was about to try and offer an explanation, but was saved by a knock at the door. Nina's savior was the person who had been the biggest protester to her marriage to Larry: Barbara.

Barbara had once again been eavesdropping outside the door. After hearing Nina's initial explanation of the circumstances surrounding the crash, she shared her brother's confusion. No matter how hard she tried, she could not figure out how Precious was able to unfasten her seat belt while underwater and get out of a badly smashed door.

"Larry, can I get you anything? Oh, hi, Nina; I didn't know you were in here."

"No, Barbara, I'm fine," Larry replied.

"Nina, can I get you anything to eat or drink?" Barbara asked reluctantly.

"No, thank you. I'd appreciate it if you'd check in on Precious. She's in her bedroom. Let her know I'll be there in a second."

"Okay," Barbara responded.

Nina used the distraction as an opportunity to change the subject. Larry had her on the hot seat, and she was getting close to her breaking point.

"Baby, you really need to eat something. Would you like me to ask the guests to leave?"

"Yeah, it's time for everyone to leave. Please tell everyone I said thank you for coming. Let them know I'll be reaching out to all of them soon."

"You should try to take a nap. I'll get you some sleeping pills. Don't worry about the guests; I'll get rid of them and clean up."

Nina helped Larry take off his shoes and then kissed him on the forehead. It was the most affection she'd ever shown Larry and he noticed. Larry received Nina's compassionate gestures with grace as he fought back the tears that spilled from his bloodshot eyes.

Meanwhile, Barbara was upstairs sitting on Precious' bed next to the confused child. Regardless of her feelings about Nina, Barbara realized that Precious was an innocent child in search of answers.

"Do you want to talk?" Precious declined Barbara's offer with a modest shake of her head. "I understand that you're probably confused about what has happened, but I want you to know you can talk to your daddy, mommy, and me if you have any questions."

"I miss my sister, Chrissy."

"I know you do, sweetheart," Barbara replied as tears streamed down her face. "We all miss Chrissy. She's not here, but you can talk to her whenever you want to. She can hear you, even though she's living with God now."

"Are you sure she can hear me when I talk to her?"

"Yes, baby, I'm sure she can hear you."

As Barbara sat on the bed with her arms wrapped around Precious, Nina stood on the other side of the partially opened door, listening. She cried silently and wished that none of this had happened.

Nina couldn't see her daughter and Barbara, but as she peered through the door she could see Precious' bed. Staring back at her was the large teddy bear that she'd slept next to every night. The bear was propped up by the pillow with her name stitched into the pillowcase.

Suddenly, Nina felt terrible about her unwillingness to bond with the now deceased child. She regretted the harsh words she'd used during the audition. She felt ashamed when she thought about her lack of compassion toward Chrissy. Nina could feel her guilt beginning to surface, and realized that she would have to summon every bit of self-control within her to keep her feelings from erupting like a volcano.

ONE WEEK LATER

"I will never forget what I saw Nina do," Val said as she sipped on her steamy hot cappuccino.

"Yeah, that was foul. She shoulda at least tried to grab that child's hand."

"Knowing Nina, the way I do, she's probably already moved on. All she can think about is her precious daughter and her new lifestyle. The entire time I was out there, all she did was brag. The shit started to get on my nerves."

"So, is she obsessed with the idea of being rich?"

"Tyrone, Chrissy's body hasn't been buried a week, and I'll bet Nina has already talked Larry into buying her a new Range Rover."

"That dude doesn't have a clue about his wife's heinous ways."

"Not a clue."

"What do you think he'd do if he knew Nina let Chrissy drown without even attempting to save her?"

"I don't know what he'd do. Based on the relationship he had with that child, he'd probably divorce Nina faster than she could say her own name. He'd probably ship her ass right back here to the 'hood. I'll bet she wouldn't be taking Precious on any auditions here."

"Doesn't she get half of his money if they get a divorce?"

"He made her sign a prenuptial agreement. She'll get something, but it won't be enough for her to retire on. She won't get any child support because Precious isn't his child. Besides, the man is a lawyer."

"I thought you said he was an agent?"

"He is an agent. But, he's a lawyer by trade. And from what I hear, a damn good one. I'm sure he will make a case against Nina that's so convincing she'd be lucky if the judge didn't make her pay *him* some money."

"You think it would go down like that?"

"I really do. Larry loved that child more than anything. He would make Nina's life a living hell if he knew what really happened during that crash."

"Hmmm," Tyrone responded.

"What are you thinkin'?"

"Well, I'm wondering what Nina would do to keep Larry from finding out."

"If it meant she didn't have to give up that house, car, and bank account, she'd probably sell her soul to the devil."

Tyrone leaned back in his chair and stared at his coffee. The steam that hovered at the surface crept into his nostrils as he raised the cup and took a sip.

"I don't know about you, but I could use a little financial assistance. It's been hard tryin' to get back on my feet; ain't many jobs out there for a convicted felon. I'm tryin' not to return to that dope game, but I'm runnin' outta patience."

Val sat there quietly. She understood where the conversation was leading. Although she didn't feel comfortable openly endorsing blackmail, she made no attempts to denounce Tyrone's devious intentions.

"I know you are gettin' tired of strippin'. To be honest, I'm tired of you goin' to that club five nights a week to shake your ass in front of a bunch of desperate men."

"I don't hear you expressing concern about me being a stripper when I bring that money in here," Val replied flippantly. Truth be told, Val was extremely tired of working at the strip club. But unless Tyrone had come up with a way to take over the financial load, she didn't care to hear his thoughts on her stripping career. "Tyrone, stop beatin' around the bush and say what's on your mind."

"Okay, I will. I believe we should get some money from Nina. We could move out of this rattrap and get something nice. Maybe we could think about havin' some babies. You know how much I want a little boy."

Val nodded her head favorably. Surprisingly, she agreed with Tyrone's idea…up until the part about the two of them making babies.

Val grew up dirt poor. As the oldest of five children in a single parent household, Val had found herself playing mother for most of her young adult life. She wanted to have a few kids of her own, but she could never envision a day when she'd allow herself to be impregnated by a man with as little ambition and potential as Tyrone.

Val had met Tyrone when they were teenagers. Tyrone

was a rising drug dealer in their Lower Ninth Ward neighborhood. As a matter of fact, he'd started hustling back in the day alongside Nina's first love, Flip. His budding drug dealing career was cut short when he was caught with nearly a kilo of cocaine.

He was able to impress Val with his fancy lifestyle, but as in many cases, when the dope money stopped coming in, Tyrone had little to fall back on. He became a great lover out of necessity, but even that was beginning to lose its luster. At one point in their relationship, Val would've been prepared to do a commercial to endorse Tyrone's sex game. The brotha was that good. However, after her leg stopped shaking and she awakened from the coma-like sleep induced by her multiple orgasms, Val usually found that the only thing she had to show for giving her body to Tyrone was a wet ass.

Tyrone sat around the house all day playing PlayStation. God had blessed him with thirty years of life, and the only thing he had to show for it were two felony convictions, washboard abs, a mammoth-size penis, five children scattered throughout the city, five different baby mamas, and a one-pack-a-day smoking habit.

Val didn't want Nina's money as much as she wanted Nina's lifestyle. The moment she'd cast her eyes on the handsome Sharrard Hogan, she immediately knew that she'd found her winning ticket to a better life.

As far as she was concerned, Tyrone could work day and night trying to figure out ways to swindle chump change from Nina. But Val had much loftier ambitions.

Sharrard was worth more money than she could ever get from Nina. Val wanted a millionaire football player, and she was going to get Nina to hook her up whether she wanted to or not.

"I already hinted to her that we would be in touch," said Tyrone.

"Oh yeah, what did she say?"

"She just stood there looking scared."

"So what do you have in mind?"

Tyrone could look at Val's facial expression and see that she was beginning to embrace his plan. "I'm thinkin' we could hit her up for some money," he said with a grin.

"How much money?"

"A few thousand dollars each month; ya know, nuthin' too much. If we ask her for a lump sum of money, she may have a hard time hiding the withdrawal from Larry. She might hesitate. But if we get a few thousand each month, it'll be easier for her to hide the withdrawals. We could get all of our bills paid and still have a little bit to play with. How much do you think Larry is worth?"

"Nina said he's worth a few million."

"Good. He won't miss a few thousand each month."

"What if Nina refuses to cooperate?" asked Val.

"She'll cooperate if she wants to keep livin' large. If she refuses, I won't hesitate to tell Larry what really happened. All you have to do is handle this exactly like I tell you. I'm gonna make the call tomorrow night."

Val wasn't sure how Tyrone would pull this off, but she decided to follow his lead. After all, besides sexing her brains out, hustling up money was the only thing Tyrone was decent at.

Normally, Larry's snoring would awaken the dead, but he fell asleep while lying on his stomach; therefore, his pillow muffled the sound.

Nina sat with her back against the headboard and her night lamp on as she finished reading the book, *Mama's Lies—Daddy's Pain*, written by her favorite male author, Brian W. Smith.

Precious was asleep in her bedroom. With Chrissy and Barbara gone and Val back in New Orleans, the house was unusually quiet at 9:00 p.m. on a Saturday.

Nina removed her reading glasses and repositioned her pillow so that it was nice and plump like she liked it. As she used her index finger to wipe the moisture from her eyelids, she heard her cell phone ring.

With her body yearning to shut down for the evening and her yawns coming at a nonstop rate, Nina let the phone ring. A few seconds passed and then the phone started buzzing, signaling that there was a voice message.

Nina stared at the ceiling for a moment, and then crawled out of bed and retrieved the cell phone from her purse. When she checked her voicemail she heard a sinister male voice singing a very disturbing tune.

"Nina's got a seeeecreeet. What would she do to keeeeep it? Nina's got a seeeeecreeeet. What would she do to keeeeep it?"

Nina closed her phone and then looked over her shoulder to see if Larry was still sleeping. He was still asleep. In fact, his snoring was getting louder. She looked at the call log on her cell phone, and noticed that the disturbing phone call came from Val's cell phone.

To avoid being heard, Nina exited the room and stood in the hallway. She dialed Val's cell phone number to find out why and who had left the message. Much to Nina's surprise, Val didn't answer the phone; Tyrone did.

"Damn, Nina, you called back quicker than I thought you would. You must like my singing."

"Tyrone, why'd you leave that message?"

"Come on, Nina; you ain't stupid. You know what's happenin'."

"What do you want?"

"For starters, I want five thousand dollars so I can get my car fixed. I'm gonna need that before Friday."

"Are you tryin' to blackmail me?" Nina asked as she tried to keep her voice low so that Larry wouldn't hear. "Where is Val?"

"I'm right here," Val said after she took the phone from Tyrone.

"Val, what's goin' on? Do you know that Tyrone is tryin' to extort money from me?"

"What's the problem, Nina? You're married to a million-aire who gives you a monthly shopping allowance. A few thousand dollars ain't shit to y'all."

"Val, you're my best friend; I can't believe you would do something this low."

"Bitch, I know you ain't tryin' to talk shit about me after what you did to little Chrissy," Val replied sharply. "I'd suggest you give him what he wants because I can't control him. There ain't no tellin' what he might say to poor Larry."

"Val, I couldn't help what happened."

"Bullshit! Have you forgotten that I was right there and witnessed the whole thing? You could've tried to save Chrissy, but you didn't. I saw everything! That child reached out to you and you ignored her hand and went for Precious."

"What did you expect me to do?" Nina asked in a low, begging tone. "My child was going to drown."

"Your child knows how to swim. Chrissy was handicapped. She was helpless. She could barely talk, let alone swim. You should've at least tried to save her first."

"Val, you don't have any children, so you don't understand. You'd have to be a mother to understand my point. As a mother, it's my instincts to save my child. You can't blame me for trying to save my child's life first."

"Is that how you really feel, Nina?"

"Yes, I do. If you had any children, you would've reacted the same way."

"Oh really?"

"Yes, really."

"Well, answer this question, Nina. If you really feel like you didn't do anything wrong, why haven't you told Larry what really went down that night?"

"It's not that simple."

"Whatever, Nina! It's as simple as you make it. Here are the simple facts as I see them. You never really liked that child from the get-go. Did you tell Larry how you used to treat her when he wasn't around? Every chance you got, you rolled your eyes and yelled at her when he wasn't there. Did you tell Larry how you treated her when she got scared and upset at that audition? Did you tell him how you called her retarded a few hours before the accident? You let your hatred for Chrissy stop you from doing the right thing."

"Oh, so you and Tyrone extorting money from me qualifies as doin' the right thing?" Nina interjected.

"No, bitch, what we're doing qualifies as karma. You watched a poor, helpless, handicapped child drown so you could save your little spoiled brat and your own sorry ass; it's that simple!"

Nina could feel her eyes filling with water. Images of the crash were swirling around in her head like debris from a tornado. She felt in her heart that she did what any mother would do, but she couldn't find the words to formulate a defense for her decision to save Precious.

Val was extremely irate at that point, and was not about to let Nina up for air.

"By the way, I haven't forgotten that you promised to make arrangements for me to fly back to Monterey so I can come to the dinner party you're giving Larry for his birthday. When you call later this week to make arrangements to send Tyrone that money, I'll need to know the status of my flight reservations."

Val hung up the phone. Nina stood there in the dimly lit hallway for a few seconds with the phone in her hand. She couldn't believe what she'd heard. In her mind, blackmail was something that happened in the movies or on some soap opera, not in real life.

"I can't believe Val is doin' this to me," Nina mumbled as she stood in the hallway leaning against the wall.

"Doing what to you?" Larry asked as he opened the door.

"Shit, Larry!" Nina shouted and took a few steps back. "You scared the hell out of me!"

"I'm sorry. I didn't mean to scare you. I was going to get a glass of water."

"Go back to bed. I'll go and get your water."

"Are you sure?"

"Yeah, baby, I'm sure. I was going to get a snack anyway."

As Nina walked into the kitchen, she thought about Tyrone's disturbing phone call. She couldn't focus. The realization that she had no one to confide in smacked her in the face. Precious was the only family she had. Val, her best friend, former best friend, was the person she usually told every piece of her personal business to. Now Val was her biggest foe.

The next closest family member was Barbara, and Nina knew that her sister-in-law wanted nothing more than to discover one of her flaws. Barbara would run to Larry faster than an Olympic track star. She would use any excuse to encourage Larry to file for divorce. Nina was between the proverbial rock and a hard place.

"Here's your water."

"Thanks, baby. So what did Val do to you?"

"Excuse me?"

"When you were standing in the hallway, you mumbled, *'I can't believe Val is doing this to me.'* What did she do to you?"

Nina had to think quickly; Larry was very intuitive. She had to be cool as she tried to tell a convincing lie.

"Oh, it's nothing."

"It must be something; you were obviously upset. What's goin' on?"

Nina thought for a few seconds and then threw out a zinger of a lie.

"Well, baby, I wasn't going to tell you this, but I was making plans to have a birthday dinner for you next Friday. I thought I'd invite some of your friends. I wanted Val to come out so that she could help me with the arrangements. When I spoke to her tonight, she said she might not be able to come. That's why you heard me saying that."

Larry smiled and gently ran his hand along the edge of Nina's cheek.

"That's nice, baby. I don't normally do much to celebrate my birthday, but a nice dinner party might help lift my spirits. Tell Val I said I'll take care of her travel arrangements. Oh yeah, let her know that I'll invite Sharrard. I'll bet she'll fly out when she hears that. Goodnight, baby."

Unbeknownst to Larry, his pestering had solved two

of Nina's initial challenges; coming up with an excuse to bring Val back out to California and getting Sharrard to the party.

"Goodnight," Nina replied as she stared at the back of Larry's head and struggled to fight back tears. The stress was starting to wear her down. "Larry, I need to tell you something."

"Tell me what?"

Nina paused for a second. Larry was a good man. Unfortunately, it had taken the death of a child before Nina opened her eyes and recognized it. Nina knew Larry would be devastated if he ever learned the truth about what really happened that evening, but she also needed to clear her conscience.

"It's about Chrissy."

"What about Chrissy?" Larry asked as he turned around to face Nina. The proverbial cat had her tongue as she tried to respond. "What's wrong, Nina? Say what's on your mind."

"I just…I just…I just want to say that I miss her. I may not have shown it all the time, but I did love her."

A tear rolled down Larry's cheek. He and Nina had been married for four months and that was the first time he'd heard her say she loved Chrissy. Larry hugged Nina and then placed her head on his chest. He gently removed the hair covering her face and started massaging her temple. Nina stared aimlessly until she fell asleep. Or maybe she deliberately retreated into a deep sleep so that she could avoid the reality of her situation. Now that she'd told him a different version of what happened, there was no turning back for Nina. A man stranded on a deserted island had never felt as alone as she did at that moment.

Nina was in trouble. Unless she could figure out a way to silence the people who were threatening to turn her life upside down, things were going to get worse; a lot worse.

Nina hired a caterer to handle the arrangements for Larry's party. The event was supposed to be simple and quick. All she wanted to do was have a nice dinner with about twenty of his friends and colleagues.

Val arrived a few hours before the party. Her relationship with Nina was so strained at this point that she caught a cab to the house from the airport rather than ask Nina to come and get her.

After spending a few moments playing with Precious, Val retreated to the guest room and took a quick nap.

Nina made arrangements for Maria to come over and babysit Precious while the dinner party ensued downstairs. Nina still didn't like the way Maria acted toward her, but Precious really enjoyed Maria's presence. As long as she stayed out of sight, Nina figured she could tolerate her nosy employee.

Everyone walked into the dining room and sat at the

long table. The table accommodated ten seats, four on each side and one at each end. Nina and Larry sat at opposite ends of the table. Sharrard and his date sat next to each other on one side along with another white couple. Larry's best friend, Terry, sat across from Sharrard next to Val. The last two seats were occupied by Larry's partner, Jim, and his wife, Susan.

"Before we start eating, I'd like to say something," Larry announced. "The last few weeks have been extremely difficult for my wife and me. There have been times when several of you tried to reach out and offer your support, but I've refused. That's why we decided to have this dinner tonight. It's sort of our way of letting our closest friends know that we appreciate you all. Everyone, please lift your glasses. I'd like to toast to friendship."

Everyone at the table lifted their glasses and in unison said, "To friendship."

The only person who didn't toast was Val. Her eyes were fixed on Nina. Her anger seeped from her pores like gas fumes from a cracked pipe.

The dinner was awesome. The caterers brought out two huge seafood trays. The trays were four levels high and contained a mixture of lobster, shrimp, scallops, sushi, and an assortment of other fish delicacies. Everyone seemed to be enjoying the evening; everyone except Val.

Although the food served tasted amazing, the vibe at the table was awkward. At times the conversation seemed strained. Larry spent the entire evening trying to make eye contact with Nina. Terry spent the entire evening trying to make eye contact with Val. Val spent the entire night trying to make eye contact with Sharrard…they all failed.

Val tried on multiple occasions to strike up a conversation with Sharrard, but he acted as if she was invisible. The only time he made eye contact with her was when he asked her to pass the salt.

Nina could sense Val's frustration. Every chance Val got to look in Nina's direction she did, but unfortunately for her, menacing stares had little to no effect because Nina refused to look at her. Still, Val didn't hide her displeasure and Nina knew she needed to address her former best friend's concerns before she exploded right there at the table.

At the end of the meal, shortly before dessert was brought out by the caterers, Nina tried to defuse the situation.

"Val, let me show you something real quick in my room before they serve dessert."

"Sure," Val replied and stood up.

The two of them retreated to Nina's bedroom and closed the door. Before Nina could comment, Val was already in a rage.

"Why didn't you tell me Sharrard had a date?!"

"Vee, I didn't know he was coming with a date."

"What do you mean, you didn't know he was dating someone? He's your husband's biggest client, and on top of that, he's datin' a damn white girl! You can't tell me you didn't know about that?"

"Honestly, Val, I didn't know. Sharrard is a playa! He has a different woman every time he comes around."

Nina's comment about Sharrard's dating habits didn't help the situation. The look on Val's face let Nina know she needed to think fast because the situation had the potential to become combustible.

"That white girl can't hold a candle to you, Val. After dessert is served and everyone goes into the living room and media room to start socializing, I'll distract her so you can get Sharrard alone. At that point, there isn't much more I can do. I promised you I'd get the two of you together; it's your job to close the deal."

Seemingly satisfied with Nina's plan, Val calmed down… for the moment. They went back into the dining room wearing the same fake smiles they had when they left.

When the eating was over and the liquor started to pour, Nina struck up a conversation with Cindy, Sharrard's blonde-haired, blue-eyed, five-foot-six, size four, all leg with very little ass, newly purchased-breast-implants-wearing date.

The fact that Nina was considering talking to this white woman was a clear indication of how much of a threat she considered Val to be at that point. It wasn't that Nina was some type of card-carrying bigot, but like so many black women, she despised white women like Cindy because their motives were so painfully obvious.

A blind man could see that Cindy was the type of white woman who'd probably spent less than one hour of her entire life talking to any black man that wasn't tending to the lawn at her family's suburban home or detailing the BMW her parents bought for her after graduating high school.

Cindy seemed like the type of white woman who came from a family that avoided contact with minorities, like a fat kid avoids diet food. Cindy's parents would have screamed if they knew she was dating a black man. Well, they may have controlled their urge to go crazy if the black man in question was a multi-millionaire and could occasionally get the family sideline seats to the biggest sporting events.

"Cindy, those shoes and that purse are fierce," said Nina.

"Thank yoooou!" Cindy replied, with a surprised look on her face. "The purse is by Marc Jacobs and the shoes are Jimmy Choo. I noticed your shoes, too: Jimmy Choo?"

"No, BCBG. But, girlfriend, let me take you into my room and show you my Jimmy Choo collection. Sharrard, you don't mind if I steal your date for a few minutes, do you?"

"Nah, you good. Y'all go ahead and talk that girl stuff."

The group began to disperse and mingle around the elegant décor as Nina and Cindy walked toward the master bedroom. Sharrard's eyes were fixed on Nina's perfectly shaped butt. Her jeans were so tight they looked painted on. Either she wasn't wearing any panties or she had on the thinnest thong ever made. Sharrard's hormones were raging. He decided at that moment that he was going to get a piece of Nina, no matter what it took. His lustful thoughts were interrupted by Larry.

"Man, I wouldn't let Cindy go with Nina. She's going to come back and want you to take her shopping once she sees all that stuff Nina has."

"Shiiiit, it don't matter what Nina shows her; I'm dumpin' her ass after tonight anyway."

"Already?"

"Yeah, dog, I gotta cut her."

"What happened?"

"Ain't nothin' happen; she just ain't my type. Man, you know me; I need a freak."

"She ain't a freak?"

"I thought she was, but somethin' ain't right about her. I tapped that ass the first day I met her, so I figured she was gonna be a nice little freaky white dime piece to add to my stable, but..."

"So she tricked you?"

"Hell yeah! She ain't freaky enough for me. I want somebody who'll let me fuck 'em in the ear, the nose, and any other place I want to stick it. That's the first white girl I've ever messed with that actually wants a nigga to put in work."

"Ha, ha." Larry chuckled. "I know that threw you off."

"Ha, ha, my ass! When she started tellin' me she was savin' certain shit for her wedding night, I knew she had to go. Besides, I'm a real nigga; you know I ain't tryin' to 'wife' no white girl. If I'm gonna step away from the sistas, it's gonna be for somethin' finer than a white chick. Now, if she was Puerto Rican, maybe I'd reconsider, because dem Puerto Rican bitches be bad."

"That's true; J.Lo is fine," Larry replied.

"Shiiit, nigga, J.Lo is fine, but I'm talkin' about somebody like Rosario Dawson."

"Is she Puerto Rican?"

"Fuck if I know. I know she looks Puerto Rican, and she's as fine as they come."

"Yeah, she is fine," Larry agreed. "But, she ain't as fine as the ultimate Puerto Rican chick."

"Who is that?"

"Do you remember Rosie Perez from the Spike Lee joint?"

"Yeah, she was off the chain!" shouted Sharrard.

"I'd drink her damn bath water. Yeah, dog, the more I think about it, I might have to piss some sistas off and marry a Puerto Rican chick. But a white chick, I don't think so."

"I don't know, dog, some of these white girls are fine as hell these days," Larry commented.

"That's true, dog; I can't lie. I swear to you, white girls these days be havin' asses like sistas," Sharrard replied.

"I don't know what they're eating these days, but you're right," Larry said.

"I believe it's somethin' in that damn fast-food. I know sistas get mad when a brotha hooks up with a white girl, but even sistas gotta admit: white girls these days got crazy booty."

"Hmmm, you better not say that too loud." Larry looked around the room to make sure no one was standing close enough to hear their discussion.

"Oh, I ain't stupid. I'd never admit that shit to a sista. You say somethin' like that to black women and they'll wanna tie a rope around a brotha's nuts and hang him from a tree."

"You ain't lying."

"Dog, the day I met Cindy, a group of sistas walked past us and looked at me like they were ready to slice my dick off. I'm tellin' you, when they see you in public with a white girl, they assume you're dissin' them."

"That's the way sistas see it," Larry said as he shrugged his shoulders, implying that he understood the black woman's viewpoint. "They figure that a black woman gave birth to you so a black woman should be good enough to be your mate."

"Man, we ain't tryin' to diss them!" Sharrard said with an annoyed look on his face. "Most niggas just wanna fuck, period. The woman could be white, black, purple, or green. Sistas automatically assume all athletes and brothas with a little money want to marry a white chick."

"You don't think there's some truth to that?"

"Hell no! Now don't get me wrong; you do have some cats that gravitate to them white chicks once they get a little cash, but not everybody.

At that point, a voice other than Larry's and Sharrard's could be heard.

"If that's the case, you should have no problem ditchin'

little Ms. Paris Hilton and gettin' with a real sista," said Val, as she stood behind Sharrard looking sexy and curvaceous in her Apple Bottom jeans.

Larry peered over his shoulder. "Oh, hey, Val, we didn't see you standing there. How much of that conversation did you hear?"

"I heard you talkin' about some fine-ass Puerto Ricans," Val replied with a sly grin. "Don't worry; I'm not going to tell Nina how you were talkin'. Besides, I happen to agree with you. I like Puerto Rican women, too."

Both Sharrard and Larry got a rise out of Val's comment. The image of an intimate session with Val and a Puerto Rican dime piece was enough to make Sharrard smile.

"Ahhhh, I'm gonna let the two of you talk," Larry said. "It seems like y'all have some things to iron out."

Sharrard watched Larry walk away. All the while he looked at Larry, Val's eyes stayed glued to Sharrard's upper torso. He wore a thin, white, form-fitting shirt. His huge pecs looked like they'd been sculpted by Michelangelo as they stuck out like two miniature mountains. Val wanted to rip off his shirt and suck on his nipples until he screamed.

Val didn't have time to revel in her perfectly timed interruption because she saw Nina and Cindy coming back into the room. She immediately grabbed Sharrard's hand and led him outside so that they could talk.

"So, what's up, Sharrard?"

"What do you mean?"

"You know what I mean. You've been actin' funny all night. Just because you're in here with ya little white friend, you don't have to act like you don't know me. I thought we hit it off when we first met."

"We did hit it off. I didn't speak because I thought you were actin' stank."

"Why'd you think that?"

"Ahhh, let's see; maybe it was the way you rolled your eyes at me when we sat down to eat."

"I think you're seeing things."

"You think?" Sharrard replied sarcastically.

"Yeah, that's what I think. I also think that you're passin' up on a great opportunity."

"Really?"

"Yep, you said you want a freak; someone that'll let you stick it wherever you want to. Well, you're talkin' to the one woman who's probably a bigger freak than you. The great thing about me is that I'm not tryin' to have your baby or latch on to you. I just want to kick it with you—no strings attached."

No bigger lies have ever been told. Val's primary goal was to snag Sharrard, by any means necessary. If that meant getting pregnant intentionally, then so be it. She even had a safety pin close by in the event the opportunity to have sex with Sharrard presented itself. Val planned to put so many holes in the condom pack that it would look like a fly swatter when he pulled it out.

Sharrard leaned against the huge white column and looked Val up and down. He was considering everything Val said and contemplating all the ways he could utilize her friendship. "So, you're a freak?"

"Did I stutter?"

"Anything I want?"

"Is that all you see me as, a sex object?"

"I ain't sayin' all that, but you said no strings attached."

"Yes, I did. But damn, can a sista get a little conversation...maybe a date or two?"

"Of course; I have no problem with that. Shit, I'm not opposed to sponsorship, if you take care of me."

"Sponsorship?"

"Did I stutter? I said sponsorship...on one condition."

"What's that?"

Sharrard looked around to make sure no one could hear. Val looked around as well, although she had no idea what he was about to say or do.

"Here's the condition. I want a threesome."

"Excuse me?" Val asked. Her tone bordered on disgust. "Are you that sprung on that white girl that you gotta throw her in the mix?"

"I'm not talkin' 'bout her."

"Well, who?"

Sharrard leaned forward and whispered, "I wanna hook up with you and your girl, Nina."

Val wasn't expecting that. She was trying desperately to move from out of Nina's shadow. She wanted bragging rights; something to throw in Nina's face. Now she'd have to share Sharrard. Things would never be right if she allowed the person she wanted to outshine the most have a crack at the man she wanted the most. Besides, Val knew that Nina was going through a sexual drought. She suspected that Nina might actually jump at the chance.

Sharrard could tell from the look on Val's face that she wasn't doing flips over the request. Still, he wanted Nina, bad. He also knew that Val wanted him, bad. Val might frown and pout, but in the end, he had the most leverage. He had the money, the lifestyle, and the penis; Val had an hourglass figure, big dreams, and a low bank account. In this case, the leverage was definitely on Sharrard's side.

Sharrard grabbed Val's chin and gave her a soft kiss on her lips. He made sure to nibble on her bottom lip just before he pulled away.

"I can take care of you. I can move you out here and set you up nice, but ain't nuthin' in life free. You need to hook that up."

"What about Larry?" Val asked.

"What about him? Are you gonna tell him? Besides, that nigga works for me. He makes his money off my money."

The negotiations were interrupted by the opening of the front door.

"Sharrard," Cindy called out. "What are you doin' out here?"

"What's happenin', baby? I'm just talkin' to my friend, Val. Val, this is Cindy."

Cindy extended her hand to shake Val's. Val looked at her extended hand and rolled her eyes so hard that it was a miracle she didn't get dizzy. She walked past Cindy's extended hand like it didn't exist and gave her a shoulder bump that nearly knocked Cindy down.

"Sharrard, did you see that?" Cindy asked. "She nearly knocked me down. What's her problem?"

"Nothin', baby; she's havin' a hard night. I'll be back in a second. I need to let Larry know we're leavin'."

Sharrard walked in the house and looked for Val. The other guests could be heard talking and laughing in the media room. Larry was in the kitchen talking to two other agents. Just as he was about to walk over and say good-bye, he looked up on the second floor and saw Nina and Val walk into the guest room.

"What's so important that we had to talk now, Val? I gave you all the time with Sharrard you needed. If you can't work something out with him, that's your problem. There ain't nothin' else I can do. The rest is on you."

"Don't get it twisted! I can handle my business."

"Good. So we're even?"

"We're even when I say we're even. I did get a chance to speak with Sharrard. He and I are going to get together, but he asked me to set somethin' up first."

"What's that?" Val paused for a second as she searched for the focus needed to say the words. Nina was getting more irritated by the second. "What do you have to set up, Val?"

"Sharrard wants a threesome, and he wants you to be in it."

"What?!" Nina shouted. "Oh hell no! I hope you told him no. I'm not getting caught up in y'all little sex games."

"You gonna get caught up in whatever I need you to get caught up in. I want that man and you're gonna help me. If that means lettin' him tap that ass, then that's what you have to do."

"I don't have to do shit!"

"Bitch, please! You'd better take that bass outta your voice. If you blow this for me, your ass will be on that stripper pole back in New Awlins by this time next week. I'ma tell Larry everything I know. I told you I'd back off when you helped me get Sharrard. This is a part of the arrangement."

As they walked out of the room and downstairs, they both saw Sharrard standing there waiting. Nina rolled her eyes and walked past. Sharrard immediately turned and looked at Val.

"Come back later on tonight around one o'clock in the morning. Call me when you get outside and I'll come down and let you in," Val whispered.

"What about Larry?" Sharrard asked.

Val led Sharrard over to a corner and told him the plan.

"He goes to bed early. It's almost nine o'clock now, so I figure everybody should be gone tonight by eleven o'clock. If you come back after midnight, he should be sleep. He sleeps real hard so there shouldn't be a problem."

"Is Nina down with it?"

"Don't worry about Nina. I already handled that. You just remember our conversation outside."

"Trust me, boo, if you pull this off for me, I'll have you set up in an apartment out here by the end of the month."

Sharrard parked his car at the foot of the hill near the entrance to the long driveway that led up to Larry and Nina's house. He walked from the car up to the front porch and leaned against one of the huge columns as he sent Val a text message alerting her that he was outside.

"Sharrard is outside. Are you ready?" Val asked Nina.

"Let's just get this over with," Nina replied in a low tone.

"Yeah, you ready," Val curtly replied.

Val walked down the hallway and peeked in Precious' bedroom to make sure she was asleep. She then tiptoed downstairs and looked in Nina's bedroom to make sure Larry was asleep. Although she really couldn't see him, she could definitely hear him. Larry snored so loud, he could be heard even with the bedroom door closed.

"Come on in," Val whispered as she stuck her head outside the front door.

Like a veteran burglar, Sharrard tiptoed inside and

darted up the stairs. The excitement of the moment made his adrenaline flow like he was playing in a football game.

"Wuz uppppp?" he asked as he walked into the guest room and saw Nina sitting on the bed.

"Shhhh," Nina admonished. "My baby is a few doors away," she whispered in a stern tone.

A few seconds later, Val came into the room. She gently closed the door and locked it.

"Everybody is sound asleep," she said as she turned and looked at Sharrard.

Val became annoyed when she noticed that Sharrard was staring at Nina. Nina had walked to the other side of the room and was looking out the window. Sharrard walked behind her and wrapped his arms around her waist.

"Don't worry; this will be our little secret," he whispered into her ear and then started gently kissing her neck.

Nina didn't move. She just stood there with her arms folded. She fought back the desire to turn around and embrace him. This felt like rape to her. She wasn't being physically forced to have sex, but in some ways, this blackmail felt just as intrusive.

While Sharrard pulled Nina's gown off, Val walked up behind him and started raising his shirt up. She started nibbling and licking his back while she reached around and massaged his huge pole. Her rock-hard nipples were pressed against his back while his rock-hard penis was lodged up against Nina's crack.

Nina tried to stay strong, but her flesh was weak. It

had been months since she'd had sex, and her willpower was weakening like a recovering drug addict forced to sleep next to a mound of cocaine.

After Nina failed to turn around, Sharrard spun her around and attacked her perky breasts. Nina didn't fight it. In fact, within moments, she was grabbing the back of his head and pressing his face into her chest.

Sharrard lifted Nina up and placed her on the bed. He then turned to Val and pushed her on the bed. The two women lay there side by side and watched as Sharrard dropped his pants.

Sharrard opened Nina's legs and commenced to using his middle and index finger on his left hand to pleasure her. Nina grimaced and squirmed at first. Sharrard had big hands. Her hole hadn't been penetrated so aggressively in a long time.

"Uhhh," she moaned.

Sharrard showed no mercy as he readied her cavern for the pounding that was soon to come. While Nina wiggled like a virgin being broken in, Sharrard reached over and opened Val's legs and used the same two fingers on his right hand to ready her. Val's hole was accustomed to such penetration. She welcomed the intrusion. Rather than run from his massive fingers, she grabbed his wrist and forced his fingers deeper.

Sharrard smiled. He was so impressed by Val's eagerness that he decided to enter her first. But not before he slid on a condom. Val saw the condom and immediately started pondering a way to get it off.

"Don't put that on; I want it raw," she begged.

"Are you crazy?" Sharrard asked.

With the condom in place, he dove into Val's moist vagina with no hesitation. As he stroked Val with all his might, he continued to finger Nina. To help control Nina's moaning, he leaned over and stuck his tongue into her mouth and let her suck on it. Within minutes, Val was climaxing and Nina was grabbing Sharrard's wrist and forcing his fingers deeper inside of her.

While Val lay sprawled across the king-sized bed, panting and enjoying the residue of her orgasm, Sharrard slid between Nina's legs and drove his rock-hard pole deep inside of her. He grabbed Nina's ankles with one hand and placed them both on his left shoulder. This position was his specialty. It allowed him to slide deeper inside his victims, rendering them helpless and Nina was no different.

With both ankles perched on Sharrard's shoulder, Nina found herself twisted partially onto her side. Sharrard used his right hand to grab her neck and pulled her body toward him. His biceps were massive. His pecs looked like someone had stuffed two miniature basketballs in his chest. His strength was too much for her. All Nina could do was bite the pillow as she unleashed enough backed-up juice to wet a beach towel. Nina came so hard that she farted.

Val chuckled as she watched Sharrard's sweat-covered upper torso shine while he dominated Nina. Her smile turned to concern when she noticed Sharrard eyes closing.

He's about to cum. I'll be damn if I'm gonna let him spill my future in her. I want that nut inside of me. Val reached down and literally pulled Sharrard's penis out of Nina.

"I want you to fuck me some more," she demanded.

"What are you doin', girl?" Sharrard asked, annoyed.

"I want you in me."

"Wait your damn turn."

"I can't wait," Val replied as she stroked Sharrard's throbbing penis.

Once his eyes started to close again, Val pulled his penis toward her until he was forced to lay prone on top of her in the bed. She kissed him for a moment and then rolled him over on his back. Once she got him down, she ripped the condom off and hopped on top of him.

"Bitch, are you crazy?" Sharrard asked.

Val acted like she didn't hear him as she mounted his pole like a jockey mounting a thoroughbred horse. She pressed down on Sharrard's shoulders and started grinding on him. An eruption was inevitable. So much so, within seconds, Sharrard could actually feel himself squirting inside of her.

He immediately tried to regain control of the situation, but Val wasn't having it. Her swollen vaginal lips locked onto his dick like a pit bull on a steak. Val could feel Sharrard's manhood deep inside her abdomen. Her body rejoiced at the feeling of his penis kneading her walls.

Any man would have been rendered helpless by her moisture, and Sharrard was no different. After a few seconds of fake machismo, he quit fighting and allowed his body to relax. Moments later, he started climaxing so hard and loud that Val had to place a pillow over his mouth.

Val pressed his shoulders down, flung her head toward the sky, and let herself go. She could feel herself getting light-headed as she climaxed like never before. She rolled her stomach and thighs like a belly dancer at the same time he climaxed, hoping that her eggs and his sperm would meet and become one.

The room was quiet for about five minutes afterwards. Nina was sitting on a chair in the corner looking out the window. Val stared aimlessly at the ceiling as she lay naked across the bed. Sharrard looked extremely upset as he paced back and forward around the room naked.

"What's wrong?" Val asked.

"Bitch, you know what's wrong! You stole my nut," Sharrard said. "I oughta beat yo ass."

"Sharrard, you need to leave…now," Nina demanded.

Sharrard rolled his eyes at Val as he put on his clothes. He didn't look her way or say another word as he slipped on his shoes. As he walked toward the door, he turned to Val and said in a sinister voice, "You think you're slick, but I got news for you. I ain't takin' care of a baby. If you're pregnant, you'd better get rid of it."

Val didn't say anything. She just sat in the bed looking dejected. Nina never once looked in Sharrard's or Val's direction. She just sat in the high-back chair and looked out of the window. Her eyes looked sad, empty.

Sharrard opened the door and tiptoed down the stairs. Like a thief in the night, he navigated through the darkness and scurried toward the front door. But what he didn't realize was that he was being watched by a set of eyes that were peering through a partially opened bedroom door.

Larry drove into the driveway wearing a smile. At first glance, it appeared that he was smiling because Nina finally let him drive the new BMW SUV he'd purchased for her; but that wasn't the case. He sprung from the driver's seat and darted to the back of the truck. The automatic latch released and the hatch opened. Larry pulled out a shiny pink bicycle, with glitter flakes and streamers dangling from the handlebars.

He ran to the front door and called out his stepdaughter's name. "Precious, come here, baby!"

With a Capri Sun in her right hand and a partially eaten chocolate chip cookie in her left hand, Precious came running to the front door. She and Larry had developed such a close bond that she was now spending more time with him than Nina.

"Close your eyes, Cutie."

"You got somethin' for me?" Precious asked as she jumped up and down.

"Yep, I got something special for you. Open your eyes."

Precious opened her beautiful little eyes and looked

at the bike. Her million-watt smile quickly turned to a frown that could only be the byproduct of a harsh memory.

Her sudden mood change surprised Larry and sent him into fix it mode.

"Precious, what's wrong? You don't like the color?"

"I like the color."

"Well, what's wrong, baby?"

"I don't know how to ride a bike."

"Baby girl, you really don't know how to ride this bike?"

"No," replied Precious in a low tone as she avoided eye contact. "My mama never got me a bike. I tried to ride a bike one time and I fell. All my friends started laughin' at me."

In true father fashion, Larry cringed at the shame he saw in the child's eyes when she admitted she couldn't ride the bike. He knelt down and grabbed the child's chin.

"We're gonna make sure no one laughs at you again. Do you want me to teach you how to ride this bike?"

"Yeah," Precious replied as the corners of her lips begin to turn upward. The smile that came forth melted Larry's heart.

Larry grabbed the new protective helmet he bought for her and resolved that he was going to forever change the child's life. "Come on, baby, we're about to make you the best bike rider in California."

Nina sat on the plush loveseat in the corner of the living room. She stared out the window and watched as Larry tried to teach Precious how to ride her bike. With

Larry struggling to keep his hand on the back of her bike seat, Precious zoomed down the driveway. It looked like Precious was starting to get the hang of it until she looked back and noticed that Larry had released the seat and she was on her own.

The look of fear on the child's face rivaled that of a black man going to a Ku Klux Klan convention. Precious' picturesque smile turned to a shriek as she turned to look forward and saw her bike heading toward the thick shrubs that lined the edge of the driveway.

"Turn your bike, baby!" Larry yelled.

Precious followed Larry's instruction, but she turned the handlebars too hard. Seconds later, the child went from learning how to ride a bike to learning how to fly. She flew headfirst over the handlebars. Fortunately, Larry had insisted that she wear that helmet; it protected her head from the impact, but she felt the might of the hard concrete.

Nina immediately jumped to her feet when she saw Precious fly through the air like a stuntwoman. She started to run outside, but stopped when she saw Larry's reaction. She's noticed that Larry and Precious had become close, but it wasn't until that moment that she realized how far they'd progressed. Their bond was taut and unabashed. Neither Larry nor Precious hesitated to show their affection and unconditional need for the other.

Nina marveled at Larry's interaction with Precious; the way he helped her up after she fell, the gentleness he displayed as he used the palms of his hands and his thumbs to wipe away the tears and dirt that covered her face.

She was equally blown away at Precious' response to Larry. A lump developed in her throat as she fought back her emotions when she saw Precious wrap her tiny arms around his neck and place her head on his shoulder as he carried her inside to care for her bleeding kneecaps.

More than three months had passed since the crash that had taken Chrissy's life. Larry continued to succeed in business and worked hard to keep Precious and Nina feeling like they were a priority to him. Unfortunately, a person's actions can only hide the pain that festers within for a short time. Larry's facial expression seemed lifeless at times. His voice seemed monotone, even faint on some occasions. Depression had set up shop in his soul, and there didn't appear to be a departure date in sight.

Nina thought about Chrissy more than she cared to admit. Visions of Chrissy's face visited her at night while she tried to go to sleep. When she did doze off, Chrissy's image forced its way into her dreams, often causing her to awaken in the middle of the night gasping for air as her heart raced and sweat trickled around the nape of her neck.

Nina viewed these constant nightmares as her conscience nudging her to confess to Larry what had really happened on that terrible stormy evening Chrissy's life was taken. He needed answers to those questions that bounced around in his head so that he could begin to move toward acceptance and then eventually closure.

Larry scurried into the kitchen with a sniffling and embarrassed eight-year-old clinging to his neck and shoulders like a scarf on a cold Chicago winter morning.

"It's gonna be all right, Cutie," said Larry as he evoked the nickname he'd given Precious, hoping that it would help comfort her.

Nina crept up to the doorway and peered into the kitchen as she watched Larry place Precious on the granite countertop and go to work on her knees like an emergency room physician caring for a car crash victim.

"This might sting, Cutie, but I have to clean your knees."

Larry used a damp towel to clean her gashed kneecaps. He then started applying bandages to her wounds. When he finished tending to Precious' injuries, she had more bandages on her knees than an Egyptian mummy.

Larry escorted the child into the media room, turned on *Finding Nemo*, her favorite movie, opened the mini refrigerator in the corner, and pulled out a huge chilled bowl. He paused for a moment to glance at Precious and then grabbed the ice cream in the freezer and put two big scoops of chocolate ice cream in the bowl.

With a level of homage usually reserved for the likes of heads of state or the leader of a monarchy, Larry served the ice cream to Precious like it was an honor.

Whatever pain Precious felt after her hard fall was

diminishing by the second as she reveled in the attention she received.

Nina surreptitiously walked over and stood near the bottom of the staircase and listened to her daughter and husband's interaction. After a few moments, she turned and walked back into the living room and reclaimed her spot on the loveseat. Tears gushed from her eyes as the guilt she harbored inside ate away at her conscience like leeches on an exposed wound. This was the worst she'd felt since the crash.

Nina's temples begin to throb as she contemplated her next move. *Larry's a good man. I can't keep lying to him about what happened; he deserves to know the truth. Even if he hates me afterward, I have to tell him about my decision to save Precious instead of Chrissy.*

Larry walked out of the front door and retrieved the bike. He was so consumed with caring for Precious that he didn't notice Nina sitting there until he came back inside and leaned the bike against the hall closet.

"Hey you! How long have you been sitting there?"

Nina wiped her tears and tried to look away as she answered, "I've been here long enough to see how you spoil her. You did all that because she fell off her bike."

"No, that's not why I did *all that* after she fell. I did *all that* because I was trying to send two very important messages to her."

"What messages were you trying to send?"

"The first message I was trying to send was that I love

her and truly care. The second thing I was trying to show her was that she is a queen who is worthy of being pampered and catered to. I want that to be the type of treatment she grows to expect from a man. As long as I'm her father, Precious will never be allowed to think that pampering is a privilege; it's her right."

The tears Nina had successfully fought back a few moments earlier started to come back with vengeance when she heard Larry's comments. This was the type of male role model she'd always wanted for Precious. Even though she'd never felt much passion toward Larry, he'd never looked so attractive to her then at that moment. Nina realized that Precious wasn't the only person who needed him; so did she.

"What's wrong?" asked Larry. "You look like you have something to say."

"Actually, I do. I want to tell you about…"

"Wait, wait! Let me say this before I forget," Larry interrupted. "I spoke to another casting director and he's agreed to meet with you about casting Precious in a McDonald's commercial. He's pressed for time so he doesn't want to do an open casting call. This will be behind closed doors with him, Precious, and you."

"When?"

"Next Saturday. I told him I'd speak to you first, to see if you were available. He's actually called me twice during the past two days to find out if I'd spoken to you about it. What do you want me to tell him?"

Nina paused for a moment. This was the closest they'd ever been to getting Precious cast in a commercial. She wasn't sure what Larry had done to pull this off, but he must have done something impressive.

Much to Nina's chagrin, thoughts of seeing Precious on television were rudely interrupted by images of Chrissy's hand sticking out of the murky water. Only minutes earlier, Nina had decided to confess to Larry, but that was before she'd learned of this new opportunity for Precious.

"Ummm, tell him we'll be there," Nina finally replied with a culpable facial expression.

"Cool. I'll call him after I get out of the shower. I gotta get cleaned up. When I drop Val off at the airport, I'm gonna hang around there for a few minutes because Barbara's plane lands about forty-five minutes after Val leaves."

"Barbara's coming today?"

"Yeah, have you forgotten? She couldn't make it to the dinner last night because of that church function she had to oversee. But she was determined to come out and spend some time with me today and give me some birthday gifts she bought. Besides, my flight to Cleveland leaves early Monday morning, so I'll be shutting it down early Sunday night. A brotha's gotta get his rest before I meet with these snakes in the grass General Managers."

"Where is Terry? When does he return to Los Angeles to start fighting crime again?"

"He must've left real early this morning. He's supposed to hang out with his ex-girlfriend today; she has an apartment across town. He took some vacation time to come to the dinner party. I believe he has another week or so before he returns. I gave him a key to get in and out, but I doubt it if you'll see much of him during the next week. He told me he'd stop by to pick up some of the clothes he left in the hall closet before he returns to Los Angeles."

Nina just looked away. She was mentally exhausted from having to deal with Val's disposition; she was not looking forward to entertaining her annoying sister-in-law.

"Oh yeah, you said you had something to say to me. What's up?" Larry asked.

"Nothing; I only wanted to thank you for taking care of Precious the way you did."

"Don't thank me. That's my daughter now. As far as I'm con-cerned, I'm simply doing what I'm supposed to do. Besides, all little girls need that. I want to set a standard that's going to be hard on her boyfriends and her husband to match when she gets older," Larry replied as he walked over and kissed Nina on the forehead.

If Larry had taken a second to look closer, he would've seen Nina's tears coming down. Her eyes turned blood-shot red as she continued sobbing and thinking about her decision to remain quiet. Her sobbing persisted until she envisioned Precious smiling on a high-definition tele-vision holding a hamburger.

Larry kept sneaking a peek at his side and rear view mirrors to see if he could catch the airport police lurking. The message on the faded sign perched on the rusted pole that was less than five feet away from his front bumper clearly stated, *No Parking In This Area.*

Larry was determined to stay put rather than spend ten minutes riding around the parking garage searching for a parking space. Besides, Barbara had already called him and confirmed that she was picking up her luggage and on her way.

Larry stopped looking for "the man" long enough to notice the laminated wallet-size photo of Chrissy that hung from his rear view mirror. When Chrissy was alive, she rarely showed much emotion. Getting her to smile in public was nearly impossible, but on the day that this photo was taken, she had smiled like never before.

A soft summer breeze swept through his window and made the photo sway. There hadn't been much of a breeze all day, but suddenly one appeared. Larry viewed that as a sign from Chrissy that she was thinking about him, too. Larry smiled as his eyes followed the picture from side to side like a man watching a dangling watch while being hypnotized.

This tranquil moment was interrupted by Barbara's loud voice. "Larry, pop the trunk!"

"Damn, that suitcase is huge! I thought you were coming for a few days, but you look like you're planning on living with us for a year," Larry said as he helped Barb put her suitcases in the trunk.

"If I wanna stay a year, I'll do that. Do you have a problem with that?"

"No, sweetie," Larry replied as he wrapped his arms around his sister and kissed her on the cheek. "You're welcome to live in my house for as long as you want."

"Umm-hmm," Barbara replied sarcastically. "You sure you don't wanna clear that statement with your wife first?"

"Don't start, Bee. We haven't gotten inside the car yet, and you're already being catty."

The drive back to the house was filled with the same idle chat that siblings go through as they try to catch up on family gossip and the whereabouts of crack-fiend cousins and under-achieving cousins.

The sun was setting as Larry pulled up to the driveway. The light from the lamp in the living room could be seen from where Larry and Barbara stood.

"Let me guess, my sister-in-law is sitting in her favorite spot, being anti-social."

"That's where she likes to sit and read. Why do you have a problem with that?"

"I don't have a problem with it. I just think it's rude to do that for hours at a time when you have company at your house."

"Barbara, spare me! You don't want to talk to her, either."

Barbara rolled her eyes and strolled into the house. Larry struggled behind her as he stumbled while trying to carry the huge bag. Barbara and Nina gave each other a cursory head nod, and then continued to act like they hadn't noticed each other.

"Where's my little Precious?" Barbara shouted.

"Be-Be," Precious yelled as she ran down the stairs and jumped into her aunt's arms. Since Chrissy's death, Barbara, much like Larry, had become emotionally attached to Precious.

Nina kept reading her magazine and ignored the pleasantries. She spent the remainder of the evening planted on the loveseat with a blanket over her lap. It was in that spot she would rest for the evening and awaken to a day she would never forget.

The next morning, Maria and Barbara sat at the kitchen table and sipped from their coffee mugs. These two women were from totally different backgrounds, but they had seemed to connect from the moment they'd met.

Everything about them was different: their race, physical build, manner of speaking, and even their child-rearing styles. Barbara was more of an old-fashioned disciplinarian. She was like that black woman in the neighborhood that lived four houses down from yours, but yelled at you and chastised you like she was your mother. And then she'd go tell your mother what she told you. Maria was more patient and slow to anger. But despite their glaring differences they had three things in common:

they loved Chrissy, they loved Larry, and they both disliked Nina.

The Sunday morning sit down whenever Barbara was in town had become a ritual for the two of them. They talked about the world, soap operas, and their favorite topic, Nina.

"Do we have everything for dinner tonight?" Barbara asked.

"Yes, but I want to go to the market one last time to pick up some fresh fruit," Maria replied. "Will you come with me?"

"Yes, we can leave around noon."

"That's fine. I'll be ready. I'm going to go and get that last load of clothes out of the dryer," said Maria as she poured out her coffee and walked into the laundry room. She took a few steps and then said, "I want to talk to you about something that happened the night of Larry's party."

"Okay," Barbara replied. "Is everything all right?"

"To tell you the truth, I don't know," Maria replied with a look of consternation on her face.

Barbara sat a few minutes longer and stared at her coffee as she wondered what Maria was talking about. She clutched the diamond cross that hung from her neck and rested at the beginning of the crease leading down to her cleavage. Images of Chrissy dominated her thoughts and sent chills down her spine. She could feel Chrissy's presence and smell her unmistakable scent.

She got up and poured her coffee into the sink. As she

headed toward the hallway bathroom to wipe her tear-covered face, she peered in the living room and saw Nina moving around.

As the Sunday morning California sunshine invaded the living room, Nina's left eye opened as her right struggled to remain shut for a few moments longer.

Something in Nina's gut told her that she would be hearing from Tyrone soon. It had been two weeks since he'd threatened to extort money from her, and Nina grew more and more anxious as she wondered when he'd harass her again.

According to the grandfather clock in the corner of the room, it was almost eleven o'clock in the morning. Nina looked out of the window and saw Larry washing his car. The gleam from the Armor All on her tires indicated that he'd already washed her car.

Precious was drawing on the sidewalk with the colored chalk Larry had purchased for her. Nina hated the fact that he let her write all over the concrete with the chalk. She thought that time-old tradition was *ghetto* and inappropriate for kids living in upper-class communities.

Nina reached over and checked her BlackBerry to see if she had missed any phone calls. The check had less to do with a desire to speak to anyone; it actually served as an indication of her fear—fear that her extorter would try to reach her.

She carried her BlackBerry around like a pacemaker. It was a gift from her husband shortly after they were wed. Only a handful of people had the phone number, and half of them rarely called. Nina knew that when the phone rang, there was a strong possibility the call was coming from Tyrone.

Like a financially strapped single parent who constantly worried how the bills were going to get paid, Nina cringed every time her cell phone rang.

Her fear must have conjured up Tyrone because his call came as if on cue.

"Nina's got a seeecreeet, what would she do…"

"Tyrone, spare me, what do you want?" Nina replied as she relinquished her prone position and sat on the arm of the loveseat.

"Damn, you just gonna cut a nigga off? I thought you liked my singin'."

"What I would like is for you to stop callin' me. I'm gonna change this damn number."

"Nah, boo, I don't think you wanna do somethin' like that. That would just piss me off."

"How much?"

"I'm glad you asked," Tyrone replied with a chuckle. "Let's see…a nigga needs a new wardrobe. I need a couple pairs of Timbs and some new jeans and shirts. So I guess about four or five thousand dollars will do."

"How about I make it an even five thousand dollars, if you agree to not call me again?"

"Come on, boo, I ain't stupid. It's gonna take a lot more than that to make a nigga drop this hustle."

"What is it gonna take, Tyrone? I'm tired of this."

"Let's see. For starters, I gotta get a crack at that ass."

"I'm not having sex with you, Tyrone, so you should think of something else," Nina said in a tone that came dangerously close to a shout. She slammed her fist against the sofa to make up for her inability to scream out loud.

Although she tried hard to keep her tone low, Nina didn't realize that at that very moment she was being secretly watched. She was under surveillance, like a predator hiding in the shadows as it stalked its prey. In this case, the entity waiting to pounce on Nina was worse than any animal in the wild; it was her sister-in-law.

Barbara stood as still as a statue in the hallway next to the entrance as she eavesdropped on Nina's phone conversation. She walked up as Nina was pressuring Tyrone for a figure, and although she couldn't hear the entire conversation, she sensed something devious was going on. Barbara took great pride in her discernment. She felt that she could spot a sneak from a mile away. Unfortunately for Nina, Barbara had branded her the family's new number one sneak. The first time she'd met Val and Tyrone at Chrissy's funeral, she had instantly realized that they were bad news.

"For me to totally disappear, it's gonna cost you about ten grand. Since I'ma good dude, I won't require you to give me the whole amount right away. I'll take that five grand you offered and you can give me the remaining five grand within the next two months. I think that's fair."

"You think that's fair, you bastard?!" Nina shouted.

"Yes, I do. I'll be in contact tomorrow to let you know where you can drop off the cash."

"Are you here?"

"Nope. But I'll be there tomorrow. So you have a day to get my money."

Realizing that her pitch had elevated, Nina turned around to see if anyone was within earshot. When she had last looked, Larry was outside waxing his Mercedes, so she wasn't that worried about him hearing. It was her sister-in-law and Maria that she was most concerned about.

If Nina had been a split second sooner, she would have seen Barbara peering into the room. Barbara pulled her head back just in time. She stood as still as possible as she wondered if Nina had seen her. She let out a quiet sigh once she heard Nina continue to talk to her antagonist on the phone.

"I'm going to go to the police, if you don't go away."

"You can go to the police if you want, but then you'd be settin' yourself up to have to explain everything that happened. You need Larry to help your little girl get her little career goin'. You can't do that Hollywood shit out there by yourself because you don't know anybody.

"If you call the cops, not only will you make Larry want to kill you for letting his baby drown, but you'll also be fuckin' shit up for your little girl. Once that nigga finds out what you did, he's gonna pull the plug on your lifestyle and stop hookin' up your little, big-headed daughter."

"You've made your point! I'll get the money."

"Oh, trust me; I'm not worried about that. I'll call you tomorrow."

"Where do you want me to bring the money?"

"I want you to bring it to my hotel room; that way we can kill two birds with one stone. Oh yeah, I want you to wear some lace panties and bring that vibrator you was tellin' Val about."

"What?"

"Don't play dumb, Val tells me everything. I know you be rationin' the pussy so much that you had to go and buy a vibrator."

"Val doesn't tell you everything," Nina replied in a spiteful tone.

"What does that mean?"

"Nothing."

"Yeah, you meant somethin'. What are you talkin' 'bout?"

"I'm not talking about anything. I'll go to the bank and get the money today. I'll call you later."

"So you tryin' to fuck wit' a nigga's head, huh? I'll tell you what. Since you wanna get flip and shit and you've already threatened me with the police, I gotta show you that you ain't dealin with some punk-ass nigga."

Nina sat motionless for a few seconds as she held the phone in her hand and tried to figure out a way out of the unenviable predicament. Short of killing both Val and Tyrone, she didn't see any solution on the horizon.

Murder wasn't merely a fleeting thought. On more than

one occasion she'd given serious thought to trying to hire someone to deal with the two of them. She would have done it herself, but she'd watched enough episodes of her favorite television show, *CSI*, to know that there were no perfect crimes; the killer always left enough clues to get caught.

She'd watched her second favorite show, *Snapped*, enough times to know that contract killings never worked out; the evidence always led back to the person hiring the killer. Nina concluded that she would have to dance to their beat a little longer until she figured out a solution.

She went into her bedroom and changed clothes and then made her way to her closet. She moved the shoe-boxes that gathered at the edge of the shelf in her closet. The boxes were empty but they served as the perfect fortress for "Ya Boy," which was wrapped in a towel and hidden behind them.

Tucked away behind the boxes was a little .22-caliber revolver. She didn't carry it with her often, but she decided to pack it to protect her from Tyrone.

Her escape from the house was almost trouble-free until she heard Barbara call her name as she prepared to walk out the door.

"Nina, where are you heading? I was about to ask you if you wanted to go to the market with Maria and me."

Why does she want to hang out with me all of a sudden?

Nina thought. "Ummm, I can't right now. Maybe later."

"Is everything okay? You look a little troubled."

"I'm okay. I have some errands to run. There are some things I forgot to take care of before Precious' audition on Monday."

Nina didn't even wait for Barbara to respond. She scurried out of the front door and darted to her car. Larry stood a few feet away, finishing up his detailing project as he watched his wife speed out of the driveway. Seconds later, Barbara came out of the house walking at a rapid pace.

"Why is everyone in such a hurry?" Larry asked.

"Oh, I'm going to the mall. Do you want to come?" Barbara asked as she opened the car door to Larry's 2000 Lexus SUV that once belonged to his deceased wife.

Barbara opened the car door and climbed in. She was determined to follow Nina, and although she wasn't sure what Nina was up to, she wanted her brother to be with her when the truth was revealed.

"Nah, you go ahead. I'm tired. I'ma go inside and take a shower."

Fortunately for Nina, her bank had recently hopped on the trend of opening for a few hours on Sundays. She went inside and withdrew five thousand dollars in cash from her savings. She could feel a lump form in her throat when she saw that she only had $565 left in the account.

She would have to come up with a damn good excuse to get five thousand dollars from Larry in a few weeks.

Barbara sat in her car like a detective on a stakeout as she waited for Nina to come out of the bank. She revved the SUV's engine and tapped her fingers on the steering wheel as she waited anxiously to catch Nina with whomever she was talking to on the phone. She deduced from the conversation she'd overheard and Nina's trip to the bank that she was delivering money to some-one.

"What are you up to, Nina?" she mumbled. "Something ain't right. I can feel it in my spirit."

As if on cue, Nina came out of the bank and got into her car. She drove out of the bank's parking lot and headed back toward the house.

"Who are you meeting up with, Nina?" she mumbled as the faint sound of Yolanda Adams' voice could be heard coming out of her speakers.

Barbara's heart raced as she followed behind Nina. She started to curse out loud when a truck pulled in front of her and caused her to lose sight of Nina's new Cadillac Escalade.

"Dammit! Where did she go?" Barbara asked as she frantically searched for Nina's car.

The traffic around Fisherman's Wharf was especially heavy at 2:00 p.m. on a beautiful Sunday afternoon. When Barbara returned to the house, Nina was already sitting in the living room.

"Hey, Bee. Where have you been?" Larry asked.

Barbara stood still for a moment as she pondered the question. "Oh, I just went for a ride."

"Ummm-hmm," Nina replied with a heavy dose of sarcasm.

Barbara ignored the snide remark and went upstairs. She looked back at Nina and thought to herself, *Yeah, heffa, I'm watching you.*

Nina gave Barbara an equally menacing glare as she thought to herself, *Yeah, heffa, I know your big ass was following me.*

The next morning, Larry left early to go to the airport to catch an early flight. Maria left early that morning as well because she only worked on Sundays, Wednesdays, and Fridays. That left Barbara at the house to assume the nanny role.

Nina hated when Barbara came to town because she took over the place. She seemed to never stop cleaning and cooking. Nina felt Barbara did it to try to make her look bad in front of Larry.

By the time Nina had awakened, Barbara had already cleaned up the house, given Precious a bath, and left with the child. There was a note on the kitchen counter saying that the two of them had gone to breakfast at McDonald's and downtown to do a little shopping.

Nina sat there alone, pondering her options. Her secret was starting to ruin her life. First, she was forced into a ménage à trois. That was followed closely by Tyrone extorting thousands of dollars from her. Nina had absolutely no one to turn to. To say she felt lost was an understatement.

Tyrone stood at the hotel window with his cell phone in his hand. Every few seconds, he would look at the phone as if that would magically make it ring.

When the call he was waiting on finally came in, it startled him.

"Hey, can you talk?"

"Is she at home right now? Is she alone?" asked Tyrone.

"Yeah, she should be," replied the caller.

"Is she going to have the five thousand dollars?" asked Tyrone.

"She has it in a bag. I saw it before I left."

Nina heard the doorbell ring and wondered who it could be. She went to the door wearing a pair of peach-colored silk pajamas. The pajama top was low-cut and short at the bottom, exposing her navel. Made from the finest silk, it hugged her upper torso where it should have and flowed with ease elsewhere. The pants had a drawstring, but were designed to sit low on a woman's waist.

Tyrone's eyes became glued to Nina's cleavage the moment she opened the door.

"What in the hell are you doing here? Why did you come to my house?" Nina asked as she peered out of the door to see if anyone outside was watching.

"I have somethin' to do tonight so I decided to come over here this mornin.' Damn, girl, you're wearin' the hell out of those pajamas."

Nina didn't reply. She was repulsed by the nature of his visit, but even in the midst of her indignation, she couldn't help but notice how ruggedly handsome Tyrone was.

Tyrone stood approximately six-feet-five inches tall. The scar on his face actually added to his bad boy image; thus, enhancing his sex appeal. His cheek- and jawbones were pronounced and his body was chiseled. The brotha was in excellent shape.

"Wait one second," Nina said as she went to retrieve the moneybag located a few feet away.

Nina returned to the door and extended her arm out to give Tyrone the travel bag that contained the $5,000 in cash. She wanted to throw the bag at him, but feared he would retaliate by carrying through with his threat to confront Larry.

"You didn't have to come here, Tyrone. I would've met you anywhere."

"I know you would have, but I wanted to see this luxurious house you're livin' in. When Val came out here, she called me every day, braggin' about your home. I wanted to check it out for myself."

"Well, you've seen where I live and you have your money, so you can leave now."

"Damn, sexy, why are you tryin' to run a nigga off? Can I at least get a tour of the place?"

"Larry will be home soon."

"Liar! Larry left this morning to go on a business trip. I also know that your little big-headed daughter isn't here. So, I got a strong feelin' you're here all alone."

"What do you want, Tyrone?"

"I want you to give me a tour of your lovely home," Tyrone responded as he forced the door open and barged inside.

He walked leisurely as he looked at the high ceilings and took a moment to admire the expensive décor. Tyrone acted like he was observing some type of expensive art collection at a ritzy gallery. Nina, on the other hand, looked as nervous as a hooker in church.

"Okay, if this is what it will take to get you to leave, I'll give you a quick tour."

"Good. Let's start with your bedroom."

"No, we will not start with my bedroom. You can see the rest of my house, but there's nothing in my bedroom for you to look at."

Nina proceeded to show Tyrone the various rooms in the massive house. When they arrived at the media/game room, Tyrone's eyes lit up. Like most men, Tyrone was impressed by the projector screen and pool table.

"I have a proposition for you."

"Tyrone, I don't have time for your games. What do you want?"

"Nah, boo, a better question is: what do you want?"

"You know what I want. I want you and Val to stop fucking with me so that my husband and I can live our lives in peace."

"I can understand that, but life ain't always that simple."

Nina sighed aloud to show her frustration and stood in the doorway with her arms folded and a serious scowl on her face.

"What do you want from me, Tyrone?"

"I want you to play me in a game of straight pool. Val told me you were a pretty good pool player."

"I'm all right."

"I'll be the judge of that," Tyrone replied as he started to rack the balls.

"If I play this stupid game, will you leave?"

"I'll do you one better. I'll leave for good."

"What does that mean?"

"That means that if you beat me in a game of pool, I'll take this money and you'll never see me again."

"Whatever! How do I know you won't show up here next week asking for more money?"

"You don't. You're gonna have to take my word for it. I'll take Val with me and you won't have to worry about either one of us."

"Yeah, right. Even if I did believe you would leave, I don't believe Val would go with you. She'd still be here becoming a thorn in my side," said Nina as she drew back her pool stick and smacked the cue ball. She sank a solid-colored ball and a striped ball, giving her the option of playing either set. She chose the striped balls.

"Good break," Tyrone said.

Nina didn't answer. She sauntered around the table with great ease and familiarity as she pondered which set of balls would be easier to knock in; thus, giving her an easy victory and a permanent departure from Tyrone's presence.

"Look, Nina, like Al Pacino said in the movie *Scarface*, *'All I have in this world is my balls and my word, and I don't break them for nobody.'*"

"So am I supposed to be impressed by the fact that you can quote a line from a movie? What does that have to do with what the two of you are tryin' to do to me?"

"It has everything to do with this situation. If I tell you I'm gonna do somethin', I'm gonna do it. My word is my bond. If I tell you I'm gonna leave and never bother you again, then I mean that. However, that goes both ways, Nina. If I say that I'll tell Larry what I know about the crash, trust me when I tell you, I will do just that."

"You've told me what I get if you lose. What happens if you win? Are you going to want even more money?" Nina asked as she sank her fifth straight shot.

With each passing minute, the green on the surface of the pool table was becoming more and more visible. Nina had already knocked down five of her six balls that remained on the table, and was hunched over as she prepared to knock down the last striped ball before she targeted the eight ball to win the game. Just as she focused on her last ball, she heard Tyrone answer her question.

"If I win, you're gonna give me some more money and a piece of that sweet ass that's staring back at me right now."

Nina took her shot as the word ass came out of Tyrone's mouth. She sank the last striped ball easily, paused, and then looked at him.

"Tyrone, stop playin'."

"Sweetheart, do I look like I'm playin'? I want some of that. I want some so bad that I'm prepared to leave town permanently if I lose. What do you have to lose? Val has already told me that you ain't been givin' Larry any lovin'. I know you don't have any dick on the side because if you did, you would have told Val, and she would have told me by now."

Tyrone walked over to Nina and stood behind her as she bent over and prepared to knock in the eight ball. He leaned over and whispered in her ear. "If I win, I want to fuck you right here on this pool table. I'm sure Val told you how good this ten-inch dick is, and yes, it's a full ten inches when it wakes up for duty."

Nina didn't move. She could feel his rock-hard penis settle in the crack of her butt, forcing the silk pajamas she wore to retreat into her crevice. Tyrone purposely allowed his manhood to glide across her left cheek as he moved away.

As hard as she tried, Nina could not hide the fact that

she was flustered. She stared intensely at the eight ball that was about twelve inches from the corner pocket. The ball was positioned close to the rail, but far enough from it that Nina had an angle that would give her a good cut shot.

Nina could still feel the remnants of Tyrone's hot breath on her neck. Without looking back at him, she said, "You got a deal."

Tyrone smiled and backed away. He looked like he'd already won the wager.

Suddenly, Nina could feel the palm of her hands getting sweaty as she tried to will the ball into the hole. *I've made this shot one hundred times. Just focus, Nina, focus.*

As she pulled back her stick, Nina heard a thud sound on the pool table. Through her peripheral vision, she could see something shiny. Tyrone had removed a chrome semi-automatic handgun from his waistband and placed it on the edge of the pool table.

He positioned the weapon away from Nina, but within eyesight.

"Why do you feel the need to do that?" Nina asked as she tried to sound calm and not look intimidated.

"Because I can," he replied. "Besides, I want you to know that I don't like it when people try to renege on bets they make with me."

Nina continued to stare at the balls on the table. She realized that he would be able to see the fear in her eyes if she glanced at him for even a second. She swallowed what little spit that remained in her mouth, drew back her stick, and cracked the cue ball. The cue ball rolled straight toward the eight ball. Nina knew she had to hit the cue ball at the perfect angle or else it would hit the railing and ricochet away from the hole. It seemed like time stood still as she waited for the two balls to strike.

Tyrone sat on a stool in the corner of the room. He seemed extremely confidant, as if he knew she'd miss the shot. He applied chalk to the tip of the stick he was going to use. Before the two balls met, Tyrone was already walking toward the table preparing to take his first shot.

The cue ball hit the eight ball flush. But it hit it flush at the wrong angle. The pressure of the moment had gotten to Nina. The eight ball brushed against the railing, causing it to get off-line. It barely missed falling in the corner pocket.

"Shit!" Nina shouted, with a look of anguish on her face.

Tyrone approached the table, chuckling. "That's the way it goes sometimes, boo."

Nina surveyed the table and saw that Tyrone would have to knock down all six balls just to get a chance to knock down the eight ball to win. Based on the positioning of Tyrone's six solid balls, Nina figured her odds of winning were still great.

"I wouldn't smile too hard. It looks like you have a lot of work ahead of you."

Tyrone chuckled once again. He looked at Nina, winked, and then asked sarcastically, "Are you gonna give me a kiss for good luck?"

Nina rolled her eyes.

"Two ball, corner pocket. You know, Nina, I've known you for a long time."

"Tyrone, shut up and take your shot! We just met when you started dating Val."

"That's when we formally met, but I've known about you for years."

"Oh really?"

"Yep," Tyrone replied as he walked around the table with the demeanor of a seasoned pool hustler. "Six ball, side pocket. I remember you from back in the day when you lived in the St. Bernard projects."

Nina looked puzzled. She didn't remember Tyrone.

"Yeah, Nina, all the niggas in my 'hood knew about your fine ass. We knew about you, even though you didn't know us. Three ball, corner pocket."

"Did you live in the projects?"

"Nah, I didn't live in the projects, but I lived a few blocks away. I even knew Flip. Seven ball, corner pocket."

Nina could feel her heart flutter when she heard those words come out of Tyrone's mouth.

"You knew my child's father?"

"Yeah, I knew Flip. Everybody knew Flip. He was tryin' to come up, just like me. I'm puttin' that one ball in the side pocket."

"Did you hustle with Flip?"

"Now that's a tough question. Four ball, side pocket."

"What do you mean?" Nina asked. She failed to notice that while he talked, Tyrone had cleared the table of all his balls. Only the eight ball remained.

"Damn, baby girl, it looks like there's only one ball left on the table," Tyrone commented. "Eight ball in the corner pocket," he said.

Tyrone closed his eyes and gently struck the cue ball with just enough force to make it hit the eight ball. The eight ball vanished into the hole and Nina's heart nearly jumped out of her chest.

"Looks like you've lost the bet, sexy."

"Double or nothing," Nina shouted as she grabbed the rack and started retrieving the balls from the pockets. She was determined to get them racked and start game number two.

Nina's eagerness to prepare the balls for a second game was stunted when she felt the coolness of Tyrone's chrome gun tickle her spine as he eased it inside of her pajama top and up her back.

"I won the bet, Nina. It's time to pay up."

Nina stood still. She thought about using one of the pool balls to hit Tyrone in the mouth, but that would do nothing to help her position. If he didn't kill her, he would definitely make her life a living hell.

As she stood there trying to decide what her next move would be, she felt her pajama bottoms fall to her ankles. Tyrone pushed her body forward, forcing her upper body on top of the pool table. A few moments later, Nina's face was pressed against the green canvas. Her normally perky breasts were flattened as they pressed against a few of the pool balls.

Tyrone parted her supple cheeks for easier access and

then slid his pole inside of her. Surprisingly, Nina's vagina was extremely wet and provided very little resistance.

"Yeah, I knew it. You haven't had any good dick in awhile; that's why you're sloppy wet. I believe you've been curious to find out if this dick was as good as Val said."

Nina didn't respond to the comments of the narcissist who was moving in and out of her. She let out a light moan as he slid his rod deeper and deeper inside.

"Umm hmm, you can try to fight it, but I know it feels good."

Tyrone started to stroke. He stroked her at the same swift pace for the next five minutes. At first Nina didn't move, but as the seconds turned to minutes, her body betrayed her. As much as she wanted him to stop, her body seemed to enjoy the encounter. Her nipples were erect and her silence was replaced by heavy breathing.

Nina's curvaceous hips, which she'd once used to mesmerize men in the strip club, became alive once again. She pushed aside the balls and lodged her manicured fingernails into the pool table canvas. Her body started moving like a snake as she took all ten inches of Tyrone's penis.

"There we go. Now you actin' right. I know this dick feels good to you. I believe that deep down you've wanted me inside you."

Nina didn't answer.

"That's okay, baby, you don't have to answer because these big sexy hips are tellin' on you."

He wasn't lying. If someone were to walk in and see this scene, Nina's attempt to convince them that this was not a fully consensual event would have been futile.

Tyrone reached down and maneuvered both of Nina's legs so that her knees were now on the green canvas of the pool table. Her shins pressed against the railings of the table, and her feet dangled helplessly. Nina's picture-perfect butt was perfectly propped up and inviting Tyrone in…and he accepted the invitation.

The scene was like something out of a porn film. Nina rocked back and forward as she moaned without shame at this point. The more she moaned, the more trash Tyrone talked.

"There we go, Ms. Nina. Work it. Show me how much you want it," Tyrone said as he grabbed Nina's hair. "I believe you missed that shot on the eight ball intentionally. Didn't you?"

Nina refused to answer. Her reluctance seemed to annoy Tyrone.

"Answer me, dammit. You missed that shot on purpose so that you can get some of this, didn't you?"

Still, she refused to answer.

Tyrone grabbed his gun and pressed it up against Nina's temple and said, "Bitch, you'd better answer me. Did you miss that shot on purpose?"

As the tears escaped from her eyes and streamed down her face, Nina said, "Yes. Yes, I missed the shot on purpose so that I could have sex with you."

Those words were all Tyrone needed to hear. His body erupted as he relieved himself all over her butt and back.

Nina scampered across the pool table like a roach. She hopped off, collected her pajama pants, and leaned against the wall as her vaginal lips throbbed uncontrollably. It had been a long time since her vagina had experienced such friction. Tyrone pulled up his pants and grabbed the moneybag.

"You never did answer my question," Nina asked.

"What question?"

"How did you know Flip? Did the two of you hustle together?"

Tyrone's eyes were glued to the contents of the bag. He counted the stacks of money as he answered.

"Flip and I hustled in the same neighborhoods. We had some of the same friends and in some cases, his friends were my enemies. For a time we struggled to control the same territory."

"We were going to get married, but he got killed. Do you remember anything about his death?"

Tyrone closed the moneybag and started to walk out of the room. He turned and took one last look at Nina as she slouched down in the corner with her chin resting on her knees and her forearms around her shins like a woman sitting on a lily pad trying not to let her legs and feet touch the water.

"I know all about the night Flip got sprayed while he was sittin' in his car with one of his homeboys."

"What happened?" Nina asked as she lifted her chin from off of her knees. This was the closest she had ever come to getting an eyewitness account of the incident.

"Flip was workin' on the wrong set. He was in total violation. He thought he could do whatever he wanted and there wouldn't be any repercussions. He pissed off the wrong people."

"What do you mean *the wrong people?* Do you know who killed my man?"

Tyrone paused for a second. He opened up the bag and stared at the money again. With a devious smile still on his face, he looked at Nina and said, "Yeah, I know. How do you think I got this tattoo teardrop?"

CHAPTER FOUR

To describe Val and Tyrone's living arrangement as uncomfortable would be an understatement. They were both so busy scheming that they rarely saw each other. Val never bothered to tell Tyrone that she was going to California to Larry's party.

When Tyrone returned from California, he crossed paths with his estranged girlfriend. As he sat in their tiny kitchen and nibbled on a bowl of noodles, he decided to confront her.

"So how was the dinner party?" Tyrone asked, his words reeking of sarcasm.

Val immediately recognized Tyrone's jealous tone and deliberately tried to avoid a confrontation. "The party was fine."

"Did you meet any interesting people?"

The question was loaded and Val knew it. No matter how she tried to avoid the discussion she realized that Tyrone knew something.

"Tyrone, what's on your mind?"

"Nothin', I'm just askin' you a question."

"Whatever."

Tyrone started to get angry at Val's reluctance to engage

in discussion. "What, you've been hangin' out in Cali so much that you're too good to answer a fuckin' question?"

"What do you really want to know, Tyrone?"

"I wanna know everything that happened while you were out there in Cali at Larry's party."

"How did you know Larry had a party? I never told you about that."

"Don't worry about how I find out about shit. Just answer the damn question. Who were you hangin' out with at the party?"

"I was with Nina."

"Bullshit!" Tyrone yelled as he slammed his fist against the small dining table.

"Since you know so damn much, Tyrone, you should tell me who I was hangin' out with."

"Okay, I will. I know your ass was hangin' out with that nigga, Sharrard. I know you were grinnin' in his damn face every chance you got. I know you went outside and was all hugged up with that ma'fucka, too."

"We were just talkin', Tyrone. Why do you always have to exaggerate shit?"

"Exaggerate? Bitch, please! You must think I'm stupid. I'm gonna give you a chance to tell me the truth before…"

"Before what? What the fuck are you're gonna do if I don't tell you the truth?"

"Don't push me, Val."

"Trust me, I don't wanna push you. If I was gonna push your sorry ass anywhere, I'd push you down to the un-employment office so you could find a damn job."

"You don't be worryin' about a nigga gettin' a job when he hittin' that ass."

"That's all you have to brag on? The fact that you have a big dick. Nigga, do you know how many big dicks they got walkin' around this country? Do you think you're the only nigga on the planet that can sling dick? Boy, you don't even know the kind of shit I got stashed in my room to take care of myself when yo ass ain't around."

By this time, Tyrone stood up and started pacing the floor. He and Val were truly made for each other. She was one of the few women he'd ever met who had a temper that rivaled his in every way.

He walked behind Val as she sat down in the chair and placed his hands on her shoulder. With the steely look of an assassin, Tyrone leaned down and whispered in her ear, "I know you fucked that dude, Sharrard. I can't prove it yet, but I know you did. You'd better hope I never find out the truth, or else I'm gonna kill you and him."

Val sat in the chair. She had about a month to figure out a way to separate from Tyrone. But now she had a problem. There was a chance she was pregnant with Sharrard's baby. Tyrone would know it wasn't his child and go on a rampage. To make matters worse, Sharrard had already told her that he wasn't taking care of a child. Val now found herself in a quagmire.

In an effort to calm him down, Val changed her tone. She leaned back and kissed Tyrone on his unshaven cheek. "Baby, I haven't been fuckin' anyone but you. I promise."

Tyrone stepped back and took a long look at Val. He

knew she was lying. He knew she'd slept with Sharrard. Most importantly, he knew Val was planning on leaving him. That kiss she'd just planted on his cheek was a dead giveaway.

He walked out of the kitchen and into the bedroom. When the door slammed behind him, it startled Val. The reverberating kick started her adrenaline and she started to contemplate her options. It wasn't long before she realized that she only had one real option, she needed to go somewhere and lay low. Somewhere Tyrone wouldn't be able to find her. Somewhere she could hide in the event she really was carrying Sharrard's baby.

Val figured that she had Sharrard by the balls if she was pregnant. One DNA test would definitely set her up financially for life. But she'd have to escape Tyrone's wrath long enough to give birth. All of this hiding would take money; money she didn't have.

Val came to one conclusion: she needed Nina's help. Nina had already siphoned money from Larry's account and participated in a threesome with one of his clients; therefore, getting her to commit to this investment shouldn't be hard. Nina was going to pay, whether she wanted to or not.

Back in Monterey, Nina prepared Precious for her big McDonald's audition in San Francisco. She spent hours helping the child study her lines the day before. On Tuesday, she had a stylist come to the house to fix her daughter's hair while she drove around the city in search of the perfect outfit for Precious.

While driving to the audition, Nina's phone started to ring. Nina looked down and saw that the call came from a restricted number. She started to let it ring, but she was waiting on a call from another talent scout. Since she didn't know the scout's phone number she felt compelled to answer the phone.

"Hello?"

"Hey, what are you doing? I need to talk to you."

"I can't talk, Val; I'm taking Precious to an audition."

"Where?'

"Why do you want to know?"

"Because I wanna know!"

Nina hesitated before she answered. "She has an audition today for a McDonald's commercial."

"That's great! Let me speak to her."

"Why?"

"Because I wanna wish her well! Now give her the damn phone," Val ordered.

Nina gave Precious the phone.

"Who is this, Mommy?"

"It's Aunt Val. She wants to say something to you."

Precious smiled as she grabbed the phone. "Hey, Aunt Val! I'm going to do a commercial for McDonald's. Mommy said they'll probably give me a free hamburger."

"They probably will, baby. I want you to do your best, but don't feel bad if you don't get it."

"Okay."

"I'm gonna see you soon."

"Are you coming out here again, Aunt Val?"

"Yeah, Aunt Val is going to move to California real soon."

"Are you going to live in our house?"

"I don't know about that, but I'll be livin' in Monterey around you. So, I'll get to see you a lot more."

"Mommy, Aunt Val says she's coming to live around us!"

Nina snatched the phone from the child. "What is she talkin' about?"

"You heard the child. I'm comin' to live in California."

"How? You don't have a job or a place to stay. You ain't living in my house."

"I didn't ask to live in your house. And no, I don't have a job, but none of that matters."

"Why not?"

"Because I got you…my friend; you're gonna sponsor me while I'm out there."

"Bullshit!"

"Yeah, bitch, you're gonna sponsor me or else."

"Or else what? You're gonna tell Larry what you know? I don't even care. Larry and I will be married one year by this time next month. The worst that can happen is that he finds out what happened and divorces me. I'll still walk away with over a hundred grand."

"Not if he finds out that you fucked his client."

"You don't have any proof. Sharrard ain't gonna confess, he can't stand you right now anyway. That means it's your word against mine."

"That's what you think."

"What does that mean?"

"That means I believe Tyrone found out what happened that night. Whoever told him will probably confirm my story."

Nina became silent. She tried to recall the events of that evening. The house was empty that night Sharrard came over. Larry was sound asleep so there was no way anyone could have known what happened.

"My, my, my. Nina Dennison is suddenly quiet. Well, let's see if you can stay quiet long enough to hear what I need you to do. I need you to help me get an apartment somewhere out there, and I need you to make this happen within the next week. I'll be in touch with you in about three days. You'd better have some answers, or I swear to you, I'm gonna call Larry."

Val hung up the phone. Nina threw the phone on the passenger seat and cursed out loud.

"What's wrong, Mommy?" Precious asked.

"Nothing, baby. Mama just has a few things on her mind. Don't worry about me. All I need you to do is focus on your lines."

They arrived at the tiny studio where the audition was held shortly before noon. Precious walked into the room like a seasoned veteran and nailed the audition. Her performance was nearly flawless. She did so well that the director started discussing future commercial opportunities right there on the spot.

"Can I have a hamburger now?" she innocently asked.

The director immediately sent an intern out to the McDonald's located a mile away to retrieve a Happy Meal for the child.

When the intern returned with the meal, he gestured for Precious to follow him into a small kitchen area. The young man walked into the room first, but he stopped and turned around when he noticed that Precious had stopped at the door.

"What's wrong?" the intern asked.

"My daddy said that men are supposed to hold the door open for women."

Everyone in the room started to laugh, including the intern. One of the female producers walked by and said to Nina, "Your husband has taught her well. I wish my daughter's father would have done the same with our child."

Nina gave a brief smile and then watched Precious from afar as she ate the hamburger. Larry had really been a positive influence on both of their lives. Nina tried to pretend she didn't care about Larry, but anyone who paid close enough attention could see that he'd slowly begun to win her over.

On the way home, Nina contemplated her discussion with Val. She decided at that moment that enough was enough. Tyrone and Val would never back off. She had to get rid of them. She had to silence them both once and for all.

The wineglass was filled to the rim with Chardonnay when Nina finished pouring. She took up residence on her favorite living room loveseat as she pondered her options for hours. She finally came up with a plan that would forever get rid of Val and Tyrone. She decided to kill them both and make it look like an accident, or even better, self-defense.

Nina's hand trembled as she made the phone call. Her stomach rumbled and her mouth failed to produce saliva. It was time to put her plan into motion. The hunted had now become the hunter.

"Hello?"

"Val, this is Nina. I took care of the arrangements."

"I'm listening."

"I reached out to someone I met out here. She manages a small apartment complex in the city of Seaside, about ten minutes from here. It's not that fancy, but she gave me a good deal on the apartment."

"When can I move in?"

"She told me she can't hold the apartment for that long, so you're going to have to move in within the next week or so."

"Good. Tell her to fax the lease to me. There's a copy store a few blocks away from here that lets you receive faxed documents. Hold on while I get the number."

"She can't fax it."

"Why not?"

"Because she said she needed you to be here to sign the lease before the move-in date. They can't start getting the apartment cleaned until you sign a lease. Besides, she's going to need a copy of your driver's license."

"I don't have a way to get there in a few days, so you need to talk to her again."

"I've made arrangements for you to fly into Monterey on Friday night. Your ticket has already been purchased. She's expecting you to come into her office on Saturday morning to sign the lease."

"That's too soon. I still need to make arrangements for my furniture."

"I've already arranged to take care of that. Didn't you say that you like my furniture?"

"Yeah."

"Well, I have an account at that store where I bought most of my stuff. I'm willing to put up to three thousand dollars' worth of furniture on that card. That should be enough to get you a bedroom set and a sofa or something. You can take care of the rest once you get here."

Val didn't reply right away. She held the phone and pondered what she was hearing. Nina was being very accommodating. Was she that scared of Larry finding out her secret or was it because she was up to something?

"All right," Val said in a low tone. "I need to figure out a way to get away from Tyrone's crazy ass. Under no circumstances do I want him to know. If he calls you asking about me, you need to tell him you don't know… if you know what's good for you."

"Of course, I'm going to pretend I don't know. Why would I deliberately try to piss you off? I'm doing this because I want all of this shit to be over and done with. The sooner I get you off my back, the sooner I can move on with my life.'

"I'm going to stick to my word and back off, but I can't promise you Tyrone will. He's on a mission."

"I'll take care of Tyrone so that he's no longer a problem for you or me. I've already made plans to have him dealt with."

Val became quiet once again. There was something in Nina's tone that she didn't like. "You said this Friday?"

"Yeah, this Friday; your flight is scheduled to leave at six o'clock on Southwest Airlines. You should land here somewhere around eight o'clock that night. I promised to take Precious to a movie, so I may not be finished in time to come and get you from the airport. Just catch a cab and come over. You can let yourself in the house. The code hasn't changed."

Nina hung up the phone and smirked. *Yeah, bitch, I have something for you. Now I just need to take care of your man.*

She waited an hour and then implemented part two of her plan.

"Hello," Tyrone said in a deep voice. He was wrapping up a brief nap that followed his argument with Val.

"Can you talk?"

"Who is this?"

"This is Nina. I need to tell you something, but I need you to be alone before I get into it."

Tyrone stood up and walked over to the door. He opened and peeked into the other room to see if Val was there. When he didn't see her in there, he looked in the bathroom and saw that it was also empty.

"Yeah, she's gone. Wuz up?"

"I need to talk to you about what happened between us."

"What about it?"

"Well, there are two things I want to tell you. The first is that…"

"Spit it out, shit! A nigga ain't got all day!"

"Well, Tyrone, I hate to admit it, but I've been thinkin' about you."

Tyrone let loose a cocky smile, grabbed the crotch of his pants, and started squeezing and rubbing his penis.

"Shit, girl, that ain't nothin' to be ashamed of. You ain't the first and won't be the last person to be thinkin' 'bout this dick after getting a piece."

Nina looked upward and rolled her eyes as she forced herself to listen to his bragging.

"I gotta admit, Tee, I did enjoy our encounter…even though I didn't want to enjoy the feeling. Since you left, I can't stop thinking about how you made me feel on that pool table. I guess that's an indication of how much my body needed that."

"Umm hmm. I knew you were likin' this pipe. What's

on your mind? You want some mo' of this dick, don't ya?"

"Yes."

"I can't hear you. Ask me to come and give you some more of this dick."

Nina rolled her eyes once again before she replied, "Tee, I want you."

"'Nah, that ain't good enough. Have you ever seen the movie *Jerry Maguire?*"

"Yes."

"Then you remember that scene when he started shouting '*Show me the money!*'"

"Yes, I do."

"Good. That's how I want you to beg me for this dick. I want you to scream I want your dick!"

"I want your dick, Tyrone."

"Bitch, is ya def? I said shout that shit."

Nina paused for a moment. She actually had to stop herself from chuckling as she thought, *This nigga thinks he's the shit. He just doesn't know he's being led to the slaughter.*

"I want some of that big black dick, Tyrone! I need your dick inside of me!"

Tyrone's penis jumped rock hard. What had started out as gentle massages of the crotch area had actually escalated to all-out masturbation. As Nina screamed out loud, Tyrone blew his load.

"Tyrone. Are you still there?" Nina asked. *I'll be damned, I think this fool is jerking off.*

"Yeah, I'm still here," he replied, his speech slurred.

Nina covered her mouth in astonishment. Tyrone was really weird. He was so weird that it seemed far more unnerving than humorous.

"Uhhh, uhhh," she grumbled.

"Nina, you there?"

"Uhhh, uhhh, shit, Tyrone."

"Are you masturbating?"

"Ummm hmm," Nina confirmed, as she covered her mouth and tried not to burst into laughter.

"Fuckin' right! That's what I'm talkin' 'bout. When you gonna give me some more of that pussy?"

"I want you to come this Friday. Larry's leaving town for the weekend."

"For sho! To show you I'm not really a bad nigga, I'll even take care of my own ticket."

Yeah, with my money, Nina thought to herself. Tyrone's arrogance was going to be the death of him. He was so busy basking in his sexual glory that he didn't pay attention to the obvious change in Nina's attitude. If he had paused just for a moment and questioned her motives, he would have noticed that she was acting suspicious. But Tyrone couldn't see past the moment. If you live by the sword, you die by the sword. Tyrone's penis was his only weapon. It was the proverbial sword he used to slay women. Now his own sword was about to be turned on him.

"Make sure you come around nine o'clock. I need to make sure I've made arrangements for Precious. When you come, I'm going to give you the rest of the money you wanted. Hopefully, we can call it even from that point."

"Yeah, maybe," Tyrone replied.

Nina noticed his reluctance to commit to backing off. His response only made her angrier and more determined to dispose of him. She was offering him her body and more money and he still wasn't satisfied.

"There's another thing I need to discuss with you."

"What?"

"It's about Val."

"What about her? We on bad terms right now anyway, so ain't much you can say about her that'll piss me off."

"She's been seeing Sharrard, the football player."

"I already knew that. She denied it when I confronted her but I know."

"Well, did she tell you she was coming to Monterey this weekend?"

"Nah, she ain't say nothin' 'bout that."

"She's coming this Friday to see him. I think he's supposed to come and pick her up Saturday morning and take her on a shopping spree in San Francisco."

Tyrone's silence was exactly the response Nina was looking for. That meant that he was seething. His ego had been bruised. When a man's ego is bigger than his thoughts, he will always react to bad news rather than respond. Tyrone reacted exactly the way Nina needed him to.

"So she's planning to go and see that fool?"

"Yeah, but she made me promise not to say anything. If she knew I was telling you her plans, she'd tell Larry what she knows about the crash. I figured you might want to know because she seems to be acting crazy lately."

"What do you mean?"

"She's been threatening to tell Larry more often. I guess I don't have to tell you that if she tells Larry, he's going to divorce me and freeze all of my money. If he freezes my accounts, you won't get another dime."

"Nah, fuck that! That bitch is playin' with my money," Tyrone said.

"She'll be here Friday night. You could throw a wrench in her plans if you come around nine o'clock that night."

"All right. We'll talk again tomorrow," Tyrone said and then hung up.

No sooner than he hung up the phone, Val opened the front door. She walked inside, rolled her eyes at him, and then threw her keys on the counter.

"Tyrone, I've been thinkin'. We need a little time apart so that we can reevaluate this relationship."

Tyrone didn't respond. He fiddled with the remote control and pretended he didn't hear her.

"Tyrone, I know you hear me! I'm getting away for a few days. I'm going to go to California this weekend to clear my thoughts."

Tyrone stopped pretending he didn't hear her. He placed the remote on the sofa next to him and then asked her, "When are you leaving?"

"I'm leaving this Friday. I'm leaving in the evening time. I'm gonna dance that morning so that I can make a little money, and take it on the trip with me. That's unless you have some money to give me."

Tyrone ignored her jab.

"That's what I thought. You ain't never got money. You're the most broke nigga I know…unless you're hustlin' somebody."

"When are you returning?" Tyrone asked.

"I don't know," Val replied and then walked into the bedroom and slammed the door behind her.

Meanwhile, Nina reclined on the loveseat and smiled as she continued to formulate her plan to eliminate her two nemeses. The house grew dark as the sun started to set. Nina got up and walked toward the kitchen. She nearly jumped out of her skin when she saw a silhouette sitting at the base of the steps.

"Oh my goodness!" Nina yelled. "You scared me! I didn't know you were still here. How long have you been sitting there?"

"Long enough to hear everything you said," the silhouette replied.

CHAPTER FIVE

Nina walked around spooked for the next couple of days. Her knees seemed weak and she could not stop vomiting. She was busted. Her plan had been discovered before she could even get it going.

That voice from the dark haunted her. She spent the next few days with a headache as she agonized over her exposure.

The lifestyle she was ready to kill over was on the verge of being taken away. Her dreams of securing a better life for Precious suddenly hinged on her ability to honor the new demands placed on her by the voice that lurked in the shadows.

She had to now wonder if Larry would leave her, or if he would feel sorry for her once he knew everything that had happened. First Val, then Tyrone, and now *this* person knew part of the story.

Nina had no idea how deep a hole she'd dug the day she decided to save her flesh and blood before she attempted to save a child that wasn't hers.

The sun rose in the east and drenched the California coastline with beautiful light on the day Val arrived in town. Nina was forced to abort her original plan and follow the strict instructions of her new puppet master.

Before she could take time to catch her breath, the beautiful sun started to set and nightfall came in and cast dark shadows that stretched for miles.

"Anybody home?" Val asked as she walked through the massive front door.

She threw the duffle bag she was carrying on the floor and propped her suitcase up against the wall, and then strolled slowly into the main part of the house. Her question was met with darkness and silence. The house seemed abandoned. Val felt around the walls until she found the light switch. She went into the kitchen and grabbed a bottle of water to quench the thirst that had been building during her travels.

"They have enough food in this damn refrigerator to feed an African village," she mumbled. "All this shit for three people, and one of them is rarely here. Just plain wasteful."

Val removed a Tupperware container full of what looked like some type of Spanish rice. Her mouth started to water as she hurried to sink her teeth into one of the meals Maria had prepared.

Val was a huge fan of Maria's cooking. She appreciated the time and effort Maria put into the preparation of her meals. With a bowl of rice and one ice-cold bottle of water in tow, Val made her way toward the staircase. She daydreamed about watching the huge television in the media room while on the airplane. She seemed relaxed as she prepared to sit back and relax like she was at the movies.

Just as she stepped on the bottom step, Val heard the front doorknob rattle. The rattle sound echoed loudly, leaving her startled. The anxiety dissipated once she saw Nina walking through the door.

"Where is Precious?" Val asked as she watched Nina walk in. "Why'd you leave the door open?"

Nina didn't reply, but she did intentionally leave the door open for someone to come in behind her.

"What in the hell is goin' on?" Val asked as the second person walked through the door.

"Damn, boo, you look like you just saw a ghost," Tyrone sneered as he walked in.

"Nina, I'm gonna ask you again. What's goin' on?"

"Let me ask you a question, Val," said Tyrone. "When were you gonna tell me you were about to bounce on me and relocate out here?"

"You bitch," Val said as she looked at Nina.

Nina couldn't reply because she was too busy trying to duck as the bowl of rice Val held flew across the room and nearly hit Nina in the head.

"You scandalous cow; you must think I'm playin' with you. That's okay, I'm gonna show you better than I can tell you. Where's my damn phone?"

"It might be here inside of your purse," Nina replied, as she held up Val's Coach purse.

"Give me my damn purse," Val shouted as she marched toward Nina.

Tyrone intercepted his angry girlfriend. His anger became unleashed as he grabbed Val by her ponytail and pulled her back toward the living room. "So you were going to leave me for that fool? Did you think I'd just let you leave like that?"

"Tyrone, let me go," Val screamed.

"Yeah, let her go, Tyrone," said a voice from behind.

It was as if God had spoken. Tyrone immediately stopped tugging on Val's hair. Once Val felt his grip loosen, she stopped fighting and trying to get away from Tyrone's clutches. Nina walked toward the living room, but just as she entered, all three sets of eyes became focused on the newest member to this gathering.

From the shadows of the hallway appeared a man—it was Larry. He wore a cold stare. He looked mad enough to kill. Larry had perfected his ability to earn millions of dollars for his clients and himself by putting forth his plans with steely resolve and a calm demeanor. With books like *The Art of War* by Sun Tzu serving as his strategic reference manual, he often meditated on the skills needed to control his temper long enough to execute his diabolical plan to punish Nina for her deceit.

One quote in particular from *The Art of War* became the foundation for Larry's modus operandi in both his business and personal lives, *"To subdue the enemy's army without fighting is the acme of skill."*

Larry had learned the art of deception by working in Corporate America with some of the most ruthless men he'd ever encountered. He had learned that a passive aggressive approach could sometimes be more effective than barking loud and telegraphing your blow. The phrase, *still waters run deep*, is more accurate than people realize; Larry was living proof.

In this case, Larry's first passive-aggressive move came when he'd deliberately turned the other cheek once he figured out that Tyrone was extorting money from Nina.

Larry was a meticulous bookkeeper. He checked his bank account balances more often than a pimp checks his hookers. As a result, he immediately noticed Nina's large withdrawal from the account he'd set up for her... an account that he still had access to.

"Larry, I'm glad you're here. Let me tell you what Nina did. And let me tell you what Tyrone has been doing, too."

"Save your breath, Val; I know everything," Larry said as he walked into the room. There was a calm and peace about him. He carried himself like Al Pacino in the movie *The Godfather*. It was controlled anger, the type of person you don't want as an opponent.

Larry walked into the kitchen and pulled out a bottle of Cognac from under the sink and a glass from the cabinet. He walked back into the living room and sat down. His silence sent chills down all of their spines.

"Yeah, Larry, go ahead and let these tricks know what time it is," said Tyrone in his typical cocky manner.

"What is he talkin' 'bout, Larry?" Nina asked.

"Larry, do you want me to tell her?" asked Tyrone.

"I want you to shut the fuck up," Larry replied as he stared at Tyrone.

"Nigga, who are you talkin' to? You must not know who you talkin' to." Tyrone finally released the handful of Val's hair and turned his attention on Larry who calmly sipped his drink.

"Trust me when I tell you, Tyrone, I know exactly who I'm dealing with. I'm dealing with a dumb-ass jail bird who's too stupid to see when he's being *played*."

"Nigga, I will never get played!" Tyrone shouted. "I'm on top of my game. I'm gonna always be on top. That's why I fucked your woman. As a matter of fact, I came here tonight to fuck your woman. Nina, did your punk-ass husband tell you about the deal we worked out?"

"What is he talking about, Larry?" Nina asked as a look of disbelief came across her face.

"Like I said, Tyrone, you're a stupid nigga. I know you had sex with my wife. And yes, I'm the one who told you to come over and get the five thousand that day. Nina, that's how Tyrone knew I wasn't at home. I called and told him no one was here. I knew he was extorting money from you. I also knew that Val was using you to get at Sharrard."

Val leaned her back against the wall and placed her hand over her mouth as she too was in disbelief.

"I've known all along that you brought Sharrard back

into my house. I saw him leaving that night. When you stuck your head in my room to see if I was asleep, I was faking. I saw him tiptoe out the door after y'all finished. I'm the one who called Tyrone and told him about the little fuck festival y'all had going on in my house right under my nose."

Larry walked toward the back of the room and opened the curtains slightly and looked out upon the back patio and yard.

"Since all of you are standing here looking stupid, I'll go ahead and let all of you out of your misery. I was here on Wednesday night when Nina invited the two of you here. What y'all don't realize is that I actually saved your lives because she was planning to get both of you over here and kill you. She was planning to make it look like self-defense.

"Nina didn't know that I was sitting here in the house when she returned from the audition with Precious. I heard her phone conversation with both of you, and told her to go through with the plan to get both of you here. I didn't bring you here to kill you. I brought you here so I could look both of you in the face and bring this charade to an end."

"So you were going to kill me, Nina?" Val asked. "Were you gonna kill me the way you killed Chrissy? Did you tell Larry about that, Nina? Did you tell Larry how you let his child die in that crash?"

Nina fell to her knees. She started crying uncontrollably.

As Val and Tyrone watched Nina lose it, Larry walked over to the back patio door and opened it. From the darkness of the backyard appeared Larry's best friend, Terry, along with two police detectives.

"Tyrone LeBlanc, you're under arrest for extortion and being a convicted felon in possession of a weapon," one of the detectives said.

Tyrone looked like he was about to shit in his pants. "Hold up," Tyrone shouted, "I have all the money. Larry, dog, I can give the money back to you."

"Don't worry about it," Larry arrogantly replied. "I wipe my ass with that little bit of money. The next time you decide to extort money, you should ask for more. You committed a felony for peanuts. What you did is the equivalent of robbing a liquor store when you should've gone ahead and robbed the bank. The sentence is the same, but the return on your investment is significantly different…you dumb ass."

The two detectives snatched Tyrone like he was a rag doll. He went kicking and yelling out of the front door. Larry then turned his attention to Val.

"You know what, Val? You are stupid," Larry said. "Un-fortunately, I am all too familiar with what really went on the night of the crash. I know how Chrissy drowned."

Nina looked up at Larry and started crying louder. Her trembling became more pronounced as she lowered her head again. Teardrops formed in Larry's eyes as he thought about his child for a brief second. But this wasn't the time or the place. Larry had a few more things to deal with before he let his emotions get the best of him.

"Val, you let your greed and jealousies cloud your judgment. I knew you were scandalous when I walked in and saw you sucking Sharrard's dick less than an hour after you met him. Did you honestly think he was gonna hook up with you after that? No man wants to 'wife' a woman who gives him head the first night he meets her. Once you do that, you officially become placed in the slut category. Women who are 'wifey' material at least learn the man's name before they start giving blowjobs."

Larry took the last sip of his Cognac, glanced over at his friend Terry and then back at Val and said, "As far as your little boy-friend, Sharrard, is concerned, he's been dealt with, too."

Larry glanced at the clock on the wall that read nine o'clock sharp.

"Let me show you what I'm talking about, Val," Larry said as he grabbed the remote from off of the counter and turned on the wall-mounted television that hung in the family room.

Our top story today is a doozy. League officials received an anonymous tip on Monday that Sharrard Hogan, the new first-round draft pick of the Los Angeles Galaxy has been using steroids and cocaine habitually for the past few months. A surprise drug test proved the anonymous tip to be true.

This story gets crazier, because Los Angeles police received a second anonymous tip that drug paraphernalia could be found inside of Hogan's brand-new Ferrari. When police checked his car, they found more than just a little paraphernalia; they found nearly a kilo of cocaine in a bag under the passenger seat.

With that much cocaine in his possession, there is a strong possibility that Sharrard Hogan may also face drug distribution charges.

Stay tuned as more information regarding the arrest of first-round draft pick, Sharrard Hogan, comes in. It looks like his pro football career is over before it really got started.

Larry turned off the television and then glared at Val. He clenched his fist and then looked at his best friend.

"Terry, get this little tramp outta my house," he said as he placed the remote back on the counter.

Terry walked over and grabbed Val by the arm. She jerked away and tried to walk out on her own. Before he could escort her out, Val decided to take one last jab at both Larry and Nina.

"Did your little wife tell you that she was about to join in on the sex that night you saw me? Did she tell you that she was in that room hiding behind the door when you came in looking for her?" Val shouted and then spat at Nina.

"Hold up, Terry; I need to say one last thing to Ms. Val," Larry said as he glanced at Nina with a disappointed look on her face. "I wasn't aware that Nina was in that room that night, but I can take solace in the fact that you said Nina was 'about to' join in on the fun that night with you and Sharrard. That tells me she didn't actually participate."

The detectives that dragged Tyrone to the police car, returned and snatched Val in the same violent manner. Terry walked past Larry and opened the back door. He gestured for someone else to come in and then stepped away.

"I'm going to the station, my brotha; call me if you need me," Terry said as he gave Larry a hug.

Barbara came walking through the door with a tear-stained face, carrying Precious. She placed Precious into Larry's arms and then walked past Nina who was still kneeling and sobbing profusely.

Precious jumped out of Larry's arms when she saw Nina on the floor crying.

"Mommy!" the child shouted. Precious hugged her mom so hard that Nina nearly fell backward. "Why are you crying, Mommy? Daddy, what's wrong with Mommy?"

Larry walked over and rubbed the child's forehead in an effort to comfort her. She wasn't crying, but it was clear that the child sensed the tension in the air.

"Your mama's okay. She's just a little sad. She's going to be okay. I promise you, I'm going to take care of her."

While her ample tears and emotions hindered Nina's speech pattern, her body compensated for what she could not say. Nina released her tight grip on Precious long enough to grab hold of Larry's leg.

Larry helped Nina to her feet and hugged her. Nina's body went limp as she cried. Her unabashed tears forced Larry's tears to flow. The love for Nina that Larry had was real. Even in the midst of this emotional storm, Larry showed her that his love was truly unconditional.

"Nina, you love your daughter just as much as I loved mine. I realize that you were in a tough situation, literally and figuratively. Once I learned the truth about what happened that night, I wrestled with whether or not to confront you. I didn't become bitter until I reflected on the way you looked me in the face on multiple occasions and lied about what happened…I felt disrespected. I felt like you disrespected my child's memory. A part of me even wanted to physically hurt you, but I could never do that. That's why I allowed Val and Tyrone to blackmail you for a while. I wanted you to pay for deliberately lying to me."

"I'm so sorry," Nina sobbed.

Larry started crying with her. He had to release his pain and support his wife, even though she'd never really extended him the same courtesy during the course of their marriage.

"Nina, I forgive you now. It's been hard, but I do."

"Why now? Why don't you hate me?"

"My sister helped me," Larry replied as he looked over at Barbara who stood a few feet away crying. "Barbara helped me see that if I'd been placed in a similar situation, I probably would have opted to save my own child first. That's not a bad thing; that's called being a parent."

At this point, Nina's tears had soaked Larry's left shoulder. The guilt she'd carried since the crash rushed out of her like the floodwaters that escaped the Gulf of Mexico and descended on the city of New Orleans.

"Please don't hate me," Nina begged.

Larry used his free hand to pick Precious up. Once he got Precious firmly positioned on his hip, he gave her a soft kiss on the cheek. He wiped the tears that spilled from Nina's eyes like water flowing from a faucet.

"Nina, I could never hate you. I hate the way you handled the situation, but I don't hate you," he whispered.

"I'm sorry you had to hear the truth from Val and Tyrone," Nina said.

Larry paused for a moment. He looked at the ground and then up at Nina. With Precious cradled in his arm, he grabbed Nina's hand and started to walk toward the door.

"Don't worry about it," said Larry.

"But you've known all this time. I'm so sorry I've caused you so much pain. I should've told you. I should've told you rather than you hearing it from Val."

"Baby, how I found out is not important. We're going to work through this."

Lugging his wife and daughter in his two arms like a person carrying grocery bags into the house, Larry walked over to Barbara and stood in front of her. Nina's body was slouched over as she cried and looked down at the floor. She was too embarrassed to look in Barbara's direction. She had been so combative toward Barbara and now she owed her a debt of gratitude because Barbara came to her defense by convincing Larry to show compassion.

Nina tried to look away, but Barbara grabbed Nina's chin and forced her to look at her.

"Nina, I'm not going to stand here and pretend like I am suddenly your biggest fan," Barbara said as she fought back her own tears. "As a matter of fact, whenever I think about Chrissy, I have to pray to keep from hating you. But believe it or not, I actually understand the difficult decision you had to make."

Barbara glanced at Larry. Her bottom lip trembled as she gave up her battle to hold back the tears and allowed them to stream down her face.

"I do love my brother, and it is very clear to me that he truly loves you. So I will always support him. I have grown to love Precious, and I'll continue to treat her like a blood relative. I'm praying that God softens my heart so that I can someday embrace you like my sister…but I'm gonna need some time."

After she laid out her true feelings to Nina so that there was a clear understanding of the status of their relationship, Barbara wrapped her arms around Nina and led her into the bedroom.

"Come on; let's get you cleaned up," she whispered into Nina's ear.

Larry stood in the living room, holding Precious.

"Don't cry, Daddy. You want me to get you something to drink?" Precious asked as she wiped her dad's face.

"No, baby. I'm fine. It's time for you to go to bed."

Larry took Precious upstairs into her room. He looked over at the bed in the corner. The pillow with Chrissy's name was still on the bed. It felt like someone had shoved a stake through Larry's heart. He wanted to cry out loud, but he couldn't. There was another child sitting there who needed him.

As he tucked Precious under the covers, Larry looked into her beautiful eyes.

"Do you know how much I love you?"

"Yes."

Larry kissed the child on her forehead.

"Are you mad at my mommy?" Precious asked.

"No, baby. Your mommy and I just have some things to talk about."

"Are you still gonna be my daddy?"

"Yes, baby, I'm gonna always be your daddy."

Precious smiled and hugged Larry's neck tighter. Her hug nearly brought him to his knees. He could feel Chrissy's spirit flow through Precious' tiny arms. Chills ran up his spine as tears ran down his face.

"Daddy," Precious whispered.

"Yes, sweetheart, what is it?"

"Do you remember that day we went for the walk in the park and you were pushing me on the swing?"

"Yes."

"Do you remember that I told you what happened on that day Mommy, Chrissy, Ms. Val, and me crashed the car?"

"Yeah, I remember."

"Did you tell Mommy what I said?"

Larry thought long and hard about that afternoon at the park with Precious. He grimaced when he thought about the way he felt when he'd learned that Nina had an opportunity to save Chrissy, but didn't try.

The images of his autistic daughter drowning with little to no hope of being saved ushered in additional thoughts; thoughts that were far more fiendish. Frown lines slowly extended from one side of Larry's forehead to the other as he recalled his decision to punish Nina for her deceit. It was clear that it would take time for this wound to heal, but Larry was determined to move on.

Larry looked deep into Precious' eyes and then kissed her forehead again and said, "I will never tell your mother that you told me everything that happened during the car crash. That will be between us. Now we have our own little secret."

BOOK CLUB QUESTIONS

1 Considering the circumstances surrounding this story line, did Nina do the right thing by saving her child or should she have saved her handicapped stepdaughter first?

2 If you were Nina and you knew that there was absolutely no way Larry could have found out what really happened in that crash, would you have told him the truth about your decision, or taken that secret to your grave?

3 This next question is for those people who emphatically say they would have saved their own child rather than the stepchild. If you felt secure and justified in your decision, but you chose not to tell your partner ALL of the details because you are afraid of upsetting him/her, aren't you guilty of being a hypocrite?

ABOUT THE AUTHOR

Brian W. Smith is the author of several bestselling novels, *Mama's Lies—Daddy's Pain, Deadbeat, Beater, and Nina's Got a Secret*. Originally self-published, *Nina's Got a Secret* made several best-seller lists; was voted to the Sankofa Literary Society's "Top 100 Books of the Decade" list; and was featured on the Oprah Book Club's "What to Read" list.

During his six-year writing career, Brian has received several awards; been a Featured Author at several literary conferences; and was named "2011 Male Author of the Year" by AAMBC.

Brian continues to expand his "literary territory" by engaging in projects outside of writing novels. He is also a member of the successful all-male literary tour, The Love Literature Tour, and is an Adjunct Professor of Creative Writing at Collin County Community College (McKinney, TX).

Brian's educational background consists of two Bachelor of Science Degrees (Business Administration and Criminal Justice) and a Master of Business Administration (MBA) from the University of Dallas. Brian is a native of New Orleans, LA, and currently lives in Dallas, Texas.

Learn more about the author at www.hollygrovepublishing.com; www.Facebook.com/HollygrovePublishing; and www.Facebook.com/AuthorBrianWSmith.